325 FIRST FIGHTS

E. L. TODD

Hartwick Publishing

325 First Fights

1

AMELIA

I just finished loading the dishes in the dishwasher when there was a knock on the door.

I assumed it was Ace. He stopped by whenever he picked up firewood at the store. The thought of him being at the door gave me a jolt of excitement. Anytime I was in the same room with him, I thought about those hot kisses we shared...and where they led to.

I pulled off my rubber gloves then opened the front door. My smile faltered when I saw the man on the other side.

It wasn't Ace.

It was Evan.

My ex-husband, Evan.

"What are you doing here?" I hadn't seen him on my doorstep in nearly a year. He never dropped by for a visit. I could barely get him on the phone for a short conversation.

He slid his hands into his pockets and sighed. "I was hoping I could take the girls out for ice cream."

He wanted to spend time with them?

Did my phone call have an impact on him?

"You do...?" I still hadn't recovered from what I'd just heard. Joy I hadn't felt in a long time surged through my body. My daughters always asked for their father, and I was tired of making excuses for him.

"Yeah." He stood in his slacks and collared shirt, obviously just getting off work for the day. His hair was cut short, and his face was hollower. He'd never been overweight before, but now he looked even leaner, probably from chasing around a woman who was barely an adult.

"Yeah...of course." I opened the door wider and allowed him inside. "Rose! Lily!"

They came running down the hall. "What, Mom?" Rose asked. She stopped when she saw her father standing in the hallway. "Daddy? Lily, Dad is here!"

"Dad!" Lily ran down the hall and crashed right into his thighs.

Evan chuckled then picked both of them up, holding them in his strong arms. "Hey, princesses."

I tried not to cry.

"Want to get some ice cream?" Evan asked.

"Yes!" Rose raised both hands in the air. "Rocky road."

"Vanilla," Lily said.

Evan carried them to the door. "I'll have them back in about an hour or so."

"Sure." My voice cracked, and I could barely contain my emotion. "Take your time."

Evan looked at me with a softened expression, showing more compassion than he had in the past year. He never cared about my tears or my depression. He just grabbed his stuff and left without looking back.

Evan finally walked out with the girls and headed down the road into town.

I watched them go from the doorway, tears running freely down my face. All I wanted was for Evan to be the same father that he was before. It took a long time for me to accept that our marriage was over, but I eventually got over it. But I could never accept Evan's abandonment of my girls.

So, in that moment, I was the happiest woman on the planet.

————

THE HOUSE WAS UNNATURALLY QUIET AND CLEAN SINCE I WAS the only one there. I finally got to sit on the couch and read while sipping a glass of wine. The night was setting over the horizon, but I didn't glance at the clock and wonder when the girls would be home.

I hoped Evan would spend as much time with them as he could.

My phone lit up with a text message from Ace.

Hey. How's it going?

I noticed he checked on me a lot more often now that Bree had her memory back. Cypress used to be the one checking in with me constantly, but now that he was trying to put his marriage back together, I wasn't as much of a priority.

I shouldn't have been a priority to begin with.

Good. You'll never guess what happened.

Rose finally cleaned up her room.

I laughed because that would never happen. *No. Evan stopped by and took the girls out for ice cream.*

Ace didn't say anything back.

I knew that meant he was walking over here. Since we lived two blocks from each other, he preferred to have conversations in person. His knock sounded on the door a few minutes later.

"It's open."

He walked in and joined me on the couch, wearing his running shorts and a t-shirt. He obviously had just gone for a hike, even though he didn't appear to be sweaty. His hair was messed up from the breeze, probably along the beach. "So, he's with them right now?"

"Yeah. He just showed up on my doorstep and took them out for ice cream."

Instead of being happy, he slowly nodded and rubbed his chin. "I'm glad he pulled his head out of his ass."

"I didn't think my conversation got to him. Didn't seem like he cared."

He rubbed his hands together and watched them glide past one another as he considered what I said. "Maybe he had a change of heart."

"He must have. Maybe his girlfriend finally loosened her claws a little."

He nodded again. "I'm glad to hear that."

"When they left, I cried for twenty minutes."

When Ace turned back to me, he wore a soft expression he never showed in front of anyone else. He seemed to drop his machismo when it was just the two of us. Other than being profoundly attracted to one another, we were obviously close friends. Bree was my best friend, but something about Ace made me feel a connection I didn't have with her. "I wish it hadn't gotten that bad to begin with."

"I'm just glad things are different now. I hope it becomes a regular thing."

"I'm sure it's the beginning of something new," he whispered. "I'm glad Evan finally had the balls to take care of his responsibilities."

"Me too."

He rested his arms on his knees and glanced at my book. "Enjoying some alone time?"

"Yeah. I'm not used to it." I laughed and set my wineglass down.

He grabbed it and took a drink. "Good stuff."

"I didn't know you liked wine."

"I like anything with alcohol in it."

Like always, I felt the tension between us. Once the conversation died out, the physical chemistry ignited. I could feel it, and I assumed he must too. Now I couldn't be alone in a room with him without thinking about those big hands all over my body. I wished he'd spend the evening watching TV with us, and when the kids went to sleep, he would hop into bed with me. I didn't just want sex, but a relationship that grew out of our loyal friendship.

But that would never happen.

I cleared my throat then grabbed my glass of wine again. "Would you like some?"

"No, I shouldn't." He patted his stomach. "No carbs after dinner."

I'd never been strict with my diet. And of course, I would never have a fit body like his. I had curves and long legs, but I certainly wasn't in shape. My muscles weren't toned, but I didn't have time to work out like everyone else. When Evan had been around, I did. But that was a luxury that disappeared the day we got divorced.

The front door opened, and Evan walked inside with the kids. "We're back."

Ace stood up, looking menacing without even trying.

I knew Ace wouldn't start anything, so I ignored him. "Did you guys have fun?" I walked to the entryway and saw the girls had messy hair, telling me they went to the beach after ice cream.

"So much fun!" Rose hugged me then walked down the hallway to the bathroom so she could clean up.

"Yeah!" Lily hugged her father. "Goodnight, Daddy."

Evan kneeled down and returned the embrace. "Goodnight, princess." He kissed her forehead before he let her go.

Once Lily was gone, it was just the three of us.

And it was awkward as hell.

Evan eyed Ace before he looked at me, slipping his hands into his pockets.

I wanted to say something to break the ice, but I couldn't think of anything. I didn't want Evan to think I was dating Ace, but it really didn't matter what he thought. It was none of his business.

Ace was the first one to do anything. He stuck out his hand to shake Evan's. "It's nice seeing you with the girls."

My heart melted on the spot, seeing Ace do something compassionate when he felt so much hatred. I knew Ace wanted to murder Evan more than anyone else, but he knew how important it was to me for Evan to be part of the girls' lives.

Evan eyed his hand before he took it. "Thanks…"

Ace stepped away again, finished with being polite.

"Well, thanks for coming by, Evan." I walked to the front door and opened it. "You know you're welcome anytime."

"Thanks." He walked with me then turned back to me. He glanced at Ace before he met my eyes again. It seemed like he wanted to say something else, but he wouldn't say anything in front of company.

Ace stepped away and walked into the living room, understanding this was a private conversation between two parents.

I stepped outside and shut the door behind me. There wasn't much point in excluding Ace because I was just going to tell him what happened anyway.

Evan brushed the corner of his mouth before he spoke. "I'm sorry I haven't been around this past year. I just—"

"I don't care, Evan." I didn't care about his excuses. I didn't want to hear about his life with his new woman.

He stilled at my rebuttal, put off by it.

"I forgive you for everything. It's in the past, and it doesn't matter anymore. I just hope that means things are gonna be different. The girls love you, Evan. Just because we aren't together anymore doesn't mean we can't be a family. You're welcome in this home anytime you want. I mean that."

His eyes softened again, and he tilted his head toward the floor. "You're being a lot nicer than I deserve."

I shrugged. "You're their father. I want this to work. That's all that matters."

He stepped back on the stone step, one foot propped higher than the other. "Are you and Ace a thing now?"

The question caught me off guard. Was our attraction so obvious that even Evan picked up on it? My initial response was to say no, but my stubbornness refused to give him an answer. "I don't ask about your personal life. You don't have any business asking about mine." He cheated on me for months and then told me he was in love with another woman the same day he moved out. I didn't have to tell him a goddamn thing.

Evan held my gaze without blinking, but he couldn't hide the hint of disappointment overtaking his features. His eyes fell slightly, and his mouth tensed as he pressed his lips tighter together. If he was jealous, he was a psychopath because he had no right to feel anything of the sort.

"Good night, Evan. Please come by whenever you want. My door is always open." I turned around and walked back into the house, holding my head high and being the strong woman I'd been born to be. When he left, I didn't show any weakness. I took the high road, refusing to let him completely destroy me. I would do the same now. I turned around when I didn't hear him say anything back.

He finally walked down the rest of the steps before he looked back at me. "Good night."

THE SECOND I WALKED INTO THE OFFICE, THE GANG CORNERED me.

"Evan came by last night?" Bree asked, hopping out of her chair.

Cypress stiffened, just as interested.

Blade kept his feet on the desk as he spun a pen around his fingers. His eyes remained on me.

Ace sat back in his chair, his massive shoulders looking powerful. He didn't look at me, his eyes focused out the window.

I assumed Ace told them the news. "Yeah. He took the girls out for ice cream." I sat at my desk, feeling my heart skip a beat in preparation for the interrogation about to follow. "He was gone for a few hours, and I know they went to the beach. The girls were happy, so that made me really happy."

Bree had made her new feelings for Evan perfectly clear, and she wasn't going to change her opinion anytime soon. "Still hate him, but I'm glad he did the right thing. Looks like your words had an impact on him."

"Apparently..." The conversation had gone so poorly, but I guess he'd spent a lot of time reflecting on our discussion.

"This better not be a drive-by," Blade said. "Because that would fuck with the girls even more."

"If that's the case, my fist will have a little talk with him," Cypress threatened.

"He'll stick around," Ace finally said. "He seemed sincere."

I knew they would never like Evan again, but they would be reasonable around him since he was still the father of my kids. "Anyway...what's new with everyone?"

"Just have restaurants to manage," Blade said. "I'm manning Olives today. Ace needs a break."

"I'm gonna take care of the café," Ace said, looking cool as he sat back against his chair.

"I'll do Amelia's Place," Bree said. "I really need to learn the ropes anyway."

"Sounds like a plan," Cypress said. "Let's break." He walked out first, Blade following behind him. Ace walked out a moment later, his arm brushing against mine as he headed to the door.

I felt the static arc between us.

When the guys were gone, Bree walked up to me. "You okay?"

"I'm fine. I'm happy, actually."

"Because of Evan?"

"Yeah. I needed my girls to know their father loved them. Our dad has been gone our whole lives, and I don't think either one of us has ever been whole since, you know?"

"I've been fine," she said. "I have you."

I smiled. "You're right. We've always had each other."

"So Ace was there last night, huh?"

My grin widened. "Nothing happened."

"Why not?"

"We agreed to stay friends. You know that."

"Why not be fuck buddies?" she asked. "I mean, it works for both of you."

"I'd set myself up for heartbreak. That's why." We'd agreed not to tell anyone about our hookup last week, so I would keep my word.

"I think you could wear him down if you really tried..."

I turned to the door. "Let it go, Bree. It's never gonna happen."

"Never say never. Don't give up."

"I'm not the kind of woman to chase a guy more than once. I told him how I felt, and he rejected me. Let's move on."

She sighed like my response was irritating.

"What?" I asked. "That would just be desperate."

"In this case, I think it would be fine."

I turned around and squinted my eyes. "Bree, are you trying to tell me something?"

Her face turned whiter than a ghost. Even her lips lost their pinkness. "No...I guess I'm used to Cypress pursuing me relentlessly. No doesn't seem to matter to him."

"But you're married. Totally different."

She shrugged then walked out the door, which was unusual for her. She usually had to have the last word in any argument.

2

BLADE

"How's it going with Bree?" I asked as I sat across from Cypress at the table. I had a dark beer sitting in front of me. I needed something strong after the long day I had, but I didn't want to get into the hard liquor.

"You know how they say marriage takes work?" He brought his glass to his lips and took a long drink, his throat shifting as he took it all down.

"Yeah," I answered.

"Well, they weren't fucking kidding." He set the beer down with a loud clunk. It tapped against the hard wood of the table.

Ace tapped his fingers against the table, his beer bubbling. He wore black jeans and a dark blue shirt, blending in with the dark background of the bar on the north side of Dolores. "That bad, huh?"

"She's just a stubborn pain in the ass." He sighed as he leaned back in his chair. "Every time we make progress, she yanks us back by bringing up what I did. It's like she's forcing herself to do it too."

"She probably develops feelings for you but then feels guilty about it," Ace said. "She forces herself to remember what you did so she doesn't fall for you again. That's my best bet."

"Did Amelia tell you that?" I asked, knowing Ace wasn't the strong and silent type. Understanding complicated emotions wasn't his forte as far as I knew. But then again, he spent a lot of time with Amelia, so what did I know?

"No," Ace answered, looking at Cypress. "But I remember what Bree said to us the first time you got back together. She was still in love with you, but she didn't want to let those emotions control her decisions. So she kept repeating to herself what you did. She'll probably do it for a long time."

"Why can't she hit her head again and forget that I cheated on her?" Cypress asked. "Totally wipe it from her memory?"

"I'll smack her upside the head for you," I said with a chuckle.

Cypress dragged his hands down his face. "She wouldn't fuck me without a condom, so I got tested the next day. When I showed her the results, she said they were irrelevant because she doesn't know what I'm up to when we aren't together." He threw his arms up in the air. "Come on. Why the hell would I live next door to her if I was chasing tail all the time?"

I shrugged as I drank my beer.

"You know what her response is to that?" Cypress asked as he tilted his head. "That I fucked someone when we were together the first time, so who knows what I'd do."

Ace chuckled. "Ouch. But that's a good point."

"I hate this," Cypress said under his breath. "I hate this

so much. I want to go back to what we were. Fuck, I miss it. I miss my wife."

"You could let it go," I suggested. "If you don't think you're gonna get anywhere with her, maybe you should just walk away."

Cypress's gaze shifted to a random point in the restaurant as he considered what I said. "No. I don't want to be with anyone else. She's worth fighting for."

"If only she could hear you say that," Ace said.

"She does hear me say it," Cypress snapped. "All the time."

"I mean candidly," Ace said. "When you're saying it to her face, she might think it's just a line. But when you're saying it to us when the girls aren't around, you know it's real."

"Then how about you tell her for me?" Cypress pressed.

"I do," I said. "I've said it to her tons of times."

"Me too," Ace said. "She just needs to believe it on her own."

"It's been two months, and nothing has changed," Cypress continued.

"Not true." I pointed my finger to the ceiling. "You got laid."

"And that's a pretty big deal," Ace said. "So don't lose all hope."

"I guess," Cypress said.

"And didn't she say she would give you seven months?" Ace said. "She also said she wouldn't sleep with anyone else. That's a pretty big sacrifice for someone who doesn't have any faith. I think you really do have a chance to make this work. You just need to tough it out."

Cypress nodded, gratitude moving into his eyes.

"Thanks. I needed to hear that. Sometimes I feel defeated, you know?"

I nodded even though I had no idea what he was talking about. "Yeah…"

"The other night, I hugged her before I went inside," Cypress said. "She hugged me back and then she kissed me. It wasn't the kind of kiss you give before you screw. It was a nice kiss. It reminded me of the way she kissed me when we both used to get home from work and finally had some time to ourselves. It was good…" His eyes shifted to the table, and a dreamy look entered his expression.

I felt bad for my friend. He was being punished for something he did a long time ago, but so much had changed after that. Cheating was pretty despicable, but he was obviously a different person now. He loved Bree with all his heart. He never gave up on her—not even now. "You'll get her back, man. I know you will."

"Yeah," Ace said. "She'll come around."

Cypress drank his beer again, his eyes still shifted elsewhere.

Ace left the table and walked to the bar to get another beer. The second he got there, a woman in a black dress came to his side, standing too close to him for a stranger. She flipped her hair then chatted him up.

"Why does Ace get all the action all the time?" I asked, not really expecting an answer.

"Because he looks like Superman."

"But we're hot too."

Cypress narrowed his eyes, a smile on his lips. "You think I'm hot?"

"No, I said *we're* hot."

"Which includes me," he said. "Therefore, you think I'm hot."

"Well, you wouldn't get laid all the time if you weren't, right?"

"I don't get laid all the time," he pointed out. "I've been in the worst drought of my life for the past eighteen months."

"But you could pick up any woman in here," I said. "If you wanted to."

Cypress shrugged. "You could too."

"So you think I'm hot now?" I asked as I pointed at myself.

"No. I just said you could pick up a woman. Not the same thing."

"Sounds like the same thing to me."

Cypress finally chuckled. "You caught me. I think you're hot."

"That's what I thought." I brushed my shoulder. "As I was saying, the women always go for Ace."

"It's because he's a bodybuilder. They like to feel protected."

"But we're ripped," I pointed out. "I don't hit the gym every day just to keep my cardiovascular system in check."

"All those superhero movies are altering women's expectations."

Ace spoke to the woman at the counter for a few minutes before he returned with his beer.

"Get her number?" I asked immediately.

He took a long time to drink his beer, keeping us in suspense before he answered, "No."

"She wouldn't give it to you?" Cypress asked in surprise.

"No," Ace answered. "I never asked for it."

"Really?" I raised both eyebrows as I looked at her. "She's pretty cute."

Ace shrugged then looked at the TV.

"Because you're seeing Lady?" Cypress asked. "Is that getting serious?"

"No," Ace answered. "I don't see that going anywhere."

"I thought she was cool," I said. "Blended into the group pretty well."

"I think she's pretty and funny, but there's not much there," Ace said.

"Does there need to be more?" I asked incredulously. "I love pretty, funny girls. They're the best."

"Bree used to be funny," Cypress said. "Until she started hating me." He rubbed his jaw, his black wedding ring contrasting against his fair skin.

"She doesn't hate you." Ace turned back to me. "What's going on with you, Blade?"

"Nothing much," I said. "I got a new TV—"

"I mean women-wise," Ace said. "You haven't seen anyone in a while."

"Oh..." Should have assumed that's what he was talking about. "Not really. It's the same shit over and over. Meet a pretty woman, take her home and have some fun, and then see her a few more times until it fizzles out... I'm over it."

"You're over getting laid?" Cypress asked in surprise.

"I'm never over sex," I said. "I'm just tired of the pattern. It's a blur."

"Maybe you need something more serious," Ace said. "Sounds like you're bored of being single."

"Isn't being in a relationship more boring?" I asked.

"No," Cypress answered immediately. "Finding the right woman you want to spend your life with is the best thing that could ever happen to you. Sex is always great. We always have fun together. There's never a dull moment."

"Eh...I don't know." I'd never met a woman that interested me enough. They were all the same, it seemed.

"You're opposed to a relationship?" Ace asked.

"No," I answered. "I've never done the relationship thing before, so I don't know if I'd like it."

"It's not bad," Ace said.

"Then why don't you do it?" Cypress asked, his eyes narrowed in slight hostility.

Ace brushed it off. "Unlike you, I like being single."

"You just blew off that hot chick," I countered.

"True," Cypress said. "That's a good point."

Ace drank his beer before responding to us. "I didn't like her. That's all. Looks aren't everything."

I laughed because I thought he was joking.

Ace didn't crack a smile.

Cypress sensed Ace's dark mood, so he changed the subject. "I'm glad Evan showed up...as much as I hate him."

"Me too," I said. "Looks like our little talk straightened him out."

"Amelia doesn't know," Ace said. "He didn't mention it to her."

"Then it'll be our little secret," Cypress said. "Amelia seems to be happy, and that's all I really care about."

"Me too," I said. "Losing a husband is bad enough. But losing the father to her kids...not cool."

"Yeah," Ace said. "I think it's only a matter of time before Evan tries to get her back."

"I highly doubt that," Cypress said. "He's having too much fun with that new adult of his."

"Nah." Ace shook his head. "He's starting to rethink his actions. I can tell."

"Well, she would never take him back," I said. "No way."

"I don't think so either," Cypress said. "She better not, not after what he did."

Ace and I both looked at him.

Cypress's face fell in guilt. "I wasn't married to Bree at the time, alright? Not the same thing."

Ace and I both cut him some slack and turned quiet.

Ace finished his beer. "I should get going. I said I would meet up with Lady."

"Me too," Cypress said. "Maybe if I play my cards right, I'll get laid tonight."

I didn't have anything to do except return to an empty house. "I'm getting tired too. I have a date with my hand."

Cypress chuckled. "TMI, man."

"And telling me you're gonna get Bree into bed isn't?" I countered.

"Good point," Cypress said. "You got me."

I USUALLY GOT A COFFEE AT THE CARMEL COFFEE CO. because it was closest to my house, but I decided to change it up and head to Carmel Coffee House instead. It was near the Hippopotamus Café and was located in an alleyway between two buildings. When I reached the courtyard, there was a fountain, walls covered with ivy and red flowers, and pots planted with exotic blossoms. There was a long line, so I pulled out my phone and waited.

When it was finally my turn, I stuffed my phone into my pocket and walked up to the counter, a twenty in my hand. The aroma of fresh coffee entered my nose, brewing right at that moment behind the counter. The glass cases showed all the homemade pastries they baked every morning.

I didn't expect to see the pretty brunette behind the counter. Her hair was thick and curled at the ends, and she had big blue eyes that contrasted against her fair skin. Diamonds were in her ears, and she wore a jean dress with a white blouse over it, looking particularly European. There were a lot of tourists around here, but I assumed she lived in the city if she was working there.

"Just woke up, huh?"

I stared at her blankly. "Sorry?"

"I asked what you'd like, but you kept staring." She smiled as she looked at me, making it clear she wasn't trying to insult me. "We all have those mornings. I had one just yesterday." She kept smiling, her teeth just as pretty as everything else about her. She was petite and curvy, and her neck particularly caught my attention. She wore a thin gold necklace with a simple bar at the end. I loved everything that I saw in front of me, from her style to her looks.

I needed to stop staring and start talking. "Sorry, didn't get much sleep last night." Not true. I slept like a baby.

"It's okay. What can I get you?"

Just the sound of her voice made me hard. I was stiffening in my jeans, subtly picturing us making out on my couch with her skirt pulled to her waist. It was a strong reaction from me, considering how bored I'd been lately. "I'll take a coffee. House blend."

She typed it into her tablet. "Room for cream?"

"I drink it black."

"$2.50."

I handed her the twenty, and she made change. When she looked down, I took advantage of the opportunity to look at her. She had a few freckles on her face.

"Here's your change." She placed the money in my open palm.

It wasn't until that moment that I recognized her subtle accent. It was definitely French. Was she from France? She had to be if she had an accent, right? Would it be stupid of me to ask?

When I didn't move, she spoke. "Did you need anything else?"

"Oh, no. Sorry." I shoved everything into my pocket and stepped away.

"Sir?"

I turned back around, hoping she'd ask for my number.

"You forgot your cup." She held up the recycled coffee cup.

"Oh...duh." I took it and smiled at her, feeling like a dumbass. "Thanks." I turned away and wanted to smack myself in the forehead. I couldn't ask her out after making the biggest idiot of myself. I wasn't smooth. I wasn't cool. I wanted to tell her that I usually was much more eloquent. She'd just caught me off guard.

It was her fault, really.

I filled my coffee then walked to work, thinking about the pretty French girl who wouldn't escape my mind. If she was French, why was she here? Maybe she was in college, and she was studying abroad. I didn't know.

But I really wanted those answers.

3

BREE

Saturday was our day off from the restaurants. We let our crew take over, knowing they could handle our absence for a day just fine. Sometimes we took Sundays off too, but usually one of us checked on a few things.

I didn't know what I was going to do with my free time. The sun was out and it was a warm day, probably because it was September. The tourists were gone, and the heat set in. During the summer season, it was usually overcast more often than sunny. But once fall came around, we had our version of a heat wave.

I opened all the windows and immediately spied on my husband next door. He was sitting on the couch in his sweatpants, reading the paper. A steaming mug of coffee was beside him, and he sipped it as he read the *Pine Cone*. He was shirtless, and his body looked particularly fine that morning.

I wouldn't mind doing this on my day off.

Dino was sitting on his blanket on the couch, his head resting on his paws.

I thought about asking Amelia if she wanted to do something with the girls, but after being a full-time single mom,
she probably wanted some downtime. Hauling the kids to
the beach or the mall probably sounded like work to her.

Would it be weird if I hung out with Cypress?

Over the past two months, I'd started to see him in a
different way. I didn't necessarily see him as my husband,
but I certainly thought of him as a friend. He was a business
partner as well, someone I trusted in a financial way.

And I did agree to consider this marriage thing with an
open mind.

I pulled out my phone and stood in the window. *You have
plans today?*

He looked at his phone on the coffee table. He immediately abandoned the newspaper and picked it up. A handsome smile stretched on his face as he typed back. *I hope I
have plans with you.*

What a flirt. *Want to take Dino to the beach?*

Depends. Will you wear a bikini?

I might.

Ooh...I'm in.

What if I wear sweatpants and a baggy shirt?

Still sexy as hell, if you ask me.

I automatically smiled then looked through the window.

His face was turned to me, and he wore the same smile.
He gave me a wave, the muscles of his arms tightening and
moving with the gesture.

I waved back. *I'll be ready in thirty minutes.*

Alright. I'll meet you outside.

WE MET IN FRONT OF MY HOUSE THIRTY MINUTES LATER. HE

was in his dark blue swim trunks and a white t-shirt. He skipped the shave that morning, but the short beard around his jaw was nice. Dino was ready to go, sniffing around without a leash.

"You never put a leash on him?"

"Sometimes. But most of the time, no. He's a good boy." Cypress whistled then started walking, telling Dino to keep up with him.

I walked beside him with my bag over my arm. I packed a blanket along with sunscreen. My swimsuit was underneath my clothes, and my shades sat on the bridge of my nose. I couldn't remember the last time I'd gone to the beach to lie around. I tagged along with the gang to play volleyball at the nets, but that wasn't the same thing.

"Want me to carry that?" Cypress asked as he looked at my bag.

"Psh. I got it."

He chuckled. "Alright."

"Did you carry my stuff when we were married?"

"We still are married," he corrected. "And no. I always ask, but you always say no."

"Sounds like me." I noticed the black ring on his left hand but didn't comment on it. I never saw him in public without it. I wondered what my wedding ring looked like. He never showed it to me, and I couldn't find it anywhere in the house.

We arrived at the beach a few minutes later and walked down the stone steps to the sand. Once we were on the beach, Dino led the way and walked faster than us, eager to get to the water and check out the other dogs.

Cypress whistled loudly, and Dino bent his ears and immediately slowed down.

"Wow, he's really trained," I said.

"You were a fierce disciplinarian when he was a puppy."

"I can't see me being stern with a dog that cute."

"You're stronger than you think."

We found a spot on the sand, and I laid out the blanket. I set my bag down then took a seat.

Cypress got comfortable beside me, his elbows resting on his knees. He wore aviator sunglasses, blending in with the crowd of beachgoers and surfers. "So, when's that dress gonna come off?"

"You've already seen me naked."

"And I would love to see you naked now."

"This isn't a nude beach."

"I'll take what I can get."

I rolled my eyes then pulled my dress off, revealing my olive-green bikini. I had been planning to take the dress off anyway, so I didn't feel like I was being flirtatious.

Cypress stared at me, but I couldn't see his eyes through his sunglasses. "That's a great color on you."

"Thanks." I waited for him to take off his own shirt.

"What?" he asked with a grin.

"Are you gonna wear that shirt all day?"

He chuckled. "Wanna see some skin, huh?"

"Well, we're at the beach, and it's a sunny day..."

He pulled his shirt over his head, revealing a perfectly ripped body that could land him on the cover of a magazine. He tossed the shirt on my bag then flexed his arm. "Is that what you wanted?"

"Yeah, minus the flex."

He chuckled then relaxed.

I lay on my stomach with my torso propped up on my arms so I could stare at the water. I brought the book I'd been reading and a bottle of iced tea, but I didn't break it out right away. Dino walked across the sand and sniffed a pile of seaweed. He lifted up his leg then pissed on the plant before he walked back to us, his tongue hanging out.

"Sit, boy." Cypress patted the corner of the blanket where Dino could get comfortable.

He immediately lay down and looked at the water, his fluffy hair blowing in the gentle breeze.

I tried not to stare at Cypress's body. I'd seen him naked plenty of times, but I really thought his physique was a work of art. Every inch was carved out of living marble. His skin was flawless, lacking any noticeable scars or blemishes. His complexion was beautiful. He was definitely a beautiful man with ruggedness around the edges.

"We used to go boogie boarding together."

"We did?" I asked in surprise.

"Yeah. Our boards are still in my garage."

"And we would do that regularly?" It was interesting learning about a past I couldn't recall. I'd had interests I never thought I would care about. I'd been boogie boarding a few times when I was younger, but it was never a regular activity.

"Probably three times a week. You weren't a big jogger, so this was the only exercise you liked to do."

"Wow. I never would have guessed."

"And we're both pretty good at it."

"That's cool."

A pair of pretty women were walking our way, both wearing string bikinis and rocking perfect bodies. Their hair blew in the wind like they were in the middle of a photo shoot and a photographer was standing off to the side.

I looked away, not wanting to see if Cypress would look or not. Anytime an attractive woman was nearby, I felt insecure. I'd never had low self-esteem about my appearance. I didn't think I was gorgeous, but I didn't have any complaints about my looks. But the second I caught Cypress with someone else, I had doubts. All the pain I felt before came flooding back even though nothing had happened.

They came closer, and the blonde turned to him, recognizing him. "Hey, Cypress. How's it going?"

"Good," he answered. "My wife and I are just enjoying the beach with our dog, Dino."

I shouldn't care that he introduced me as his wife, but I did.

"Bree, this is Mandy. She works at the Anthropologie in the mall area."

I smiled and waved. "Hi. Nice to meet you."

"You too," she said with a fake smile. "Well, see you later." She walked off with her friend, their asses shaking as they moved across the sand.

Cypress returned to staring at the ocean.

I shouldn't have felt jealous, but I did. He'd cheated on me once, and I wondered what went through his mind anytime an attractive woman was nearby. Had he thought about screwing Mandy? Had she hit on him while he was married to me? Those were the kinds of questions that never went through my mind before. I didn't use to care if Cypress looked at another woman because I was confident in our relationship. I never thought he would want to be with anyone else besides me.

But now everything was different.

Cypress detected my mood change. "Please don't push me away."

I stared at the water, watching the waves rise before they fell and reached up on land. "I don't like the person I turn into when I feel this way."

He changed positions and lay on his stomach beside me. "What does that mean?"

"I get jealous and insecure. I feel ugly and petty. I wonder what you're thinking when a hot woman appears. I wonder if you'd rather be with her instead of me."

He bowed his head.

"I never used to think those things before..."

"I know."

"I never used to care if you even checked out a woman in front of me."

"Not that I ever did."

"But if you did, I wouldn't care. I never went through your phone. But now I wonder how you know her and if anything has ever happened between you two."

He played with the sand with his fingertips, finding a piece of wood and using it to draw. "One of the reasons I was attracted to you was because of your confidence. It's always been a turn-on for me. You've never shown an ounce of insecurity. I feel terrible that I've changed all of that. But I know you can conquer it and return to the way you used to be— I've seen it with my own eyes."

I couldn't picture that ever happening.

"I met Mandy when I went shopping for Amelia's birthday present. We run into each other around town, and she comes into the restaurants a lot. She's hit on me before."

"She did?" I shouldn't be surprised. Cypress was the most handsome man I'd ever met.

"Yeah."

"I'm guessing you weren't wearing your wedding ring."

"Actually, I was. She never asked if I was married, but I'm sure she knew."

"And then what happened?"

"Nothing. I told her I was married, and that was the end of it."

I'd never had anyone close to me lie to my face before that I knew of. So I naturally wanted to believe him, but there was a warning in my heart. "I wish I could believe you... I really do."

He sighed in disappointment. "I've never lied to you, Bree. I've always been honest with you."

"I don't think cheating qualifies as honest."

"But I would have told you if you hadn't caught me."

"We'll never know what would have happened." I kept my eyes on the water, not wanting to look at him.

"I would have told you. I made a mistake, but I would have been honest about it."

There was no guarantee of that. "I'm not trying to make you feel bad. I just don't think I can believe you."

He sighed again. "I guess I can understand that. But the more time you spend with me, the more you'll know who I am now. I'm the most committed guy on the planet. I'm not trying to make this work out of obligation because we're married. I'm trying to make this work because there's no other woman I want to be with. Mandy could ask me out a million times, but I'm always going to want you instead. I know it's hard to believe after what I did, but I'm truly different now. All I want is to be married to you, to make love to you every night, and to grow old with you."

It was sweet. So sweet that it gave me shivers down my spine.

"I'll never be able to apologize enough times for what I did. I'll never be able to take back that horrific night. But I'm willing to spend the rest of my life trying to make it up to you, to make you understand that you're truly the only woman I ever want to be with." He turned my way and stared at me, his eyes scorching through his shades.

"I believe you, Cypress."

"Thank you."

"There're a lot of things I like about you. I see all of your good qualities. There are times when I forget about the past, when you're holding me in front of the house. But then the memories sink back in... I think they'll always sink back in."

"They won't," he whispered. "You got through it the first time. You can do it again."

"I don't know... It'd be easier if we just moved on from each other."

"That's not an option for me," he said. "I can't fall in love with someone else. I don't want to, not when I know you're the woman I'm supposed to be with."

"I'm not saying this to make you feel bad, but if I were the woman you were supposed to be with, that never would have happened."

"You're right. But I was a different guy back then, as I've already said. I spent the entire year thinking about who I was and what I lost. I matured. I changed. Now I am who I am—and I'm better for it. Now I'm ready to be the man you should have had to begin with—if you'll give me another chance."

"Cypress...I don't know."

"I'm not asking you to do anything but try. We can keep being friends. We can keep taking it slow. Trust is something that takes a long time to be rebuild. I can be patient. Just try to see me for who I am now—and not who I used to be."

"Wanna come over and have some lunch?" We stopped in

front of our pair of houses. Dino was tired from running around at the beach all day. He ran out into the water to retrieve his ball, but once he was back on land, he was ready for another throw. After walking up the hill, he was seriously pooped out.

I didn't have anything else to do for the day, and my stomach was rumbling. After our painful conversation on the beach, the tension turned heavy, and Cypress was eager to make it easygoing again. When I didn't think about those horrible things, I really did enjoy his company. The offer was tempting. "Whatcha gonna make?"

He smiled. "How about turkey sandwiches and salads?"

"Ooh...that sounds delicious and reasonably healthy."

"They're gonna have crispy slices of bacon, so I don't know how healthy they'll really be."

I shrugged. "Healthy is overrated anyway."

We walked into his house and entered the kitchen. Dino was so tired he didn't even care about having food. He hopped onto his blanket on the couch and immediately closed his eyes.

"Wow, he's tired," I noted.

"He's used to me being at work all day." Cypress opened the fridge and pulled out all the deli meat, cheese, and produce. "He's getting fat."

"Hey, that's not true," I said. "He's not fat."

Cypress chuckled. "He's definitely chunky."

"Not true either." I pouted my lips in sadness.

"Sweetheart, you know I'm kidding. I just like to tease him." He grabbed a bag of bread and set it on the counter.

I liked it when he called me sweetheart. It was always at times when he was most affectionate. But I wondered if it was an endearment he threw around to other women.

Before those dark thoughts could sink in, I stopped thinking about them.

"Everything on it?"

"Yeah, sure. Can I help?"

"Yeah." He nodded to the fridge. "How about you take care of the salads?"

"Got it." I opened the fridge and got to work. He had leafy greens, ripe tomatoes, cucumbers, and peppers, fresh from the farmer's market in town. Silently, we worked side by side. I wondered if we used to do this sort of thing when we were married, activities that husbands and wives did on a daily basis.

When we were finished, we sat at the kitchen table near the window that overlooked his backyard and my house. The sun was still out and blinding, only a few clouds moving past as the afternoon progressed.

Cypress sat across from me and ate with both arms on the table. His gaze was usually directed outside, but he looked at me occasionally. His t-shirt was back on, so his beautiful physique was hidden from view, but his toned forearms looked nice every time he moved. His black wedding ring always caught my attention because it was so dark in comparison to the rest of his skin.

"Why black?" I finally asked.

He eyed his wedding ring, figuring out what I was talking about. "I just liked it. I didn't want anything gold."

"What's it made out of?"

"Soft metal." He pulled it off his finger and set it on the table so I could look at it. "It's comfortable. I usually don't take it off because I hardly notice it. It doesn't rust in the shower. I haven't been wearing it that long, but it doesn't dull easily. I get a lot of compliments on it too."

When women weren't hitting on him. "I like it. What

does my ring look like?" I assumed he had it because I hadn't found it anywhere in the house.

He took a bite of his sandwich.

I waited for him to answer me, knowing he'd heard what I said.

He chewed slowly before he finally swallowed. "I'll show you sometime."

"Why don't you just show me now?" Did he lose it? "Do you have it?"

"Yeah, I have it."

I waited for more.

But he wouldn't give me anything else.

"Cypress?"

"I'll give it to you when the time is right." He quickly changed the subject. "What do you think everyone else is doing today?"

When I thought about Ace, I wanted to tell Cypress the truth about Amelia, but I had to keep my promise. "I suspect Ace is hanging out with Amelia. Probably got lunch or something."

"Yeah, maybe. We went out last night, and some woman made a pass at him. But he said he wasn't interested. Honestly, I don't understand that guy."

Now I was seriously being tested, and I wasn't sure if I could restrain myself. "Is he still seeing Lady?"

"He said they hook up, but it's nothing serious. And it'll never be serious."

Ace was making it so obvious. I wish everyone else would pick up on it the way I did. "Don't you think it's strange that Ace spends so much time with Amelia and doesn't have anything serious with anyone else?"

He shrugged before he kept eating. "At first, I did. But then he said he didn't see Amelia. Why would he lie?"

Ugh. Cypress was still too dense to figure it out. "True. But maybe something is holding him back..."

"If it were anything, it would probably be the fact that he would have to be a stepfather. That's not a big perk for a lot of guys."

Oh, forget it. I paid attention to my food and looked out the window.

Cypress finished his sandwich then watched me as I took my last bites. His blue eyes were so pretty they were dangerous. They carried both mystery and intensity, having the ability to set my teeth on edge with just a simple look.

I looked down and avoided his stare, not wanting to be such easy prey. It was embarrassing how powerful his effect was on me considering everything we'd been through.

"Your backyard needs some work. I've neglected it because it was too difficult, but I'll get started again tomorrow."

"Can't we just get a landscaper?"

"We could. But I don't mind doing it myself."

I wouldn't mind seeing him work in my backyard with his shirt off. Sounded like a nice afternoon. "I can help you."

"Nah. I'd rather you sit inside and sip iced tea."

And watch you like a hawk.

I finished my lunch then carried the dishes to the sink. When my back was turned to him, I took a moment to look out the window and stare at my own house. If I didn't get out of there soon, I'd end up in his bed. I was certain of that.

I rinsed the plates then set them in the sink. "I should get going. I have—"

Cypress grabbed my arm and turned me around before he crushed his mouth to mine. His powerful body pressed me into the counter, and he closed me in by gripping the edge of the counter on either side of me. He kept me in place, his mouth secured over mine in a fiery embrace.

I should have known this would happen.

Cypress tilted my head back with his mouth and kissed me harder, his body pushing right against my tits so I could feel his thundering heartbeat. His hand left the counter then slid into my hair at the back of my head, the place where he usually grabbed me.

Once I felt that touch, I was gone.

All opposition was distinguished. All I could think about was that powerful mouth against mine, that tight body against me. When he slipped his tongue inside, my spine melted like butter on the hot stovetop.

My arms circled his neck, and I pulled him closer into me, needing more of that kiss. Like fire and gasoline, we ignited the second we were combined together. The heat spread quickly, growing in intensity until we were both burned and crisp. Nothing could stop us now, just the way humankind couldn't stop a storm.

My hands reached for his shorts, and I unfastened them before I pulled his shirt over his head. Rock-hard and solid, he had the sexiest physique in the world. I couldn't blame women for hitting on him even though he was married, not when he was so hot. My fingers trailed over his grooves of muscle, feeling the dips along his abs.

He pulled my dress off and immediately yanked on the string behind me, making my bikini top come loose. All the windows were open, but hopefully none of the neighbors was looking our way.

Once my top was gone, he grabbed one of my tits and gave it a hard squeeze, his mouth never breaking apart from mine. My bottoms were strings as well, so he pulled on those until my second piece fell to my feet.

Now I was naked in his kitchen, but I didn't feel like I was on display. His powerful body covered mine, his ass rock-hard and tight. I pulled down his shorts so he was naked with me. His long cock was throbbing in desperation, and it rested against my stomach and rib cage, twitching slightly.

Cypress stopped kissing me and lifted me into the air until my legs were wrapped around his waist. He walked into the bedroom and kicked the door shut behind him just before Dino could dart inside.

He dropped me on the bed then climbed on top of me. The shades were pulled closed so we had our privacy. The picture frame I noticed the last time I was there was still on the nightstand where he kept his watch.

My head hit the pillow, and he crawled on top of me, his powerful body blanketing mine. He separated my thighs with his knees, and he held his torso above me, his eyes focused on my mouth.

I wanted to feel that enormous dick stretch me, but he was missing something. "Condom."

He froze on top of me, his eyes narrowed in hostility. "No."

"No?" Did he really just say that to me?

"I got tested. I'm clean."

"At that point in time, yes."

"You're gonna have to give me the benefit of the doubt, sweetheart."

"Actually, I don't have to do anything."

He pressed his head inside me anyway.

"Whoa." I grabbed his hips and steadied him and tried to ignore how good he felt. "Why is it so important to you?"

"Because I don't want latex to separate us. We're husband and wife. I want to make love to you the right way. I want to feel you the right way. If I wear something, it's like I'm not inside you at all."

"But—"

He shoved himself inside me when he felt my objection waver, overpowering my grip on his hips and entering me. He held my gaze as he did, sliding his thick cock into home base.

"Oh god…" It felt a million times better when there wasn't anything separating us. His cock moved past my bare skin, sliding though my slickness with ease. I could feel the enlarged head of his cock as it pushed deeper inside me.

"You still want me to wear a condom?" He had the most arrogant smirk on his mouth I'd ever seen.

I locked eyes with him and gripped his wrists.

"Tell me, sweetheart." He rocked his hips slowly, pushing all the way inside before he pulled out again.

My mind was totally in the gutter now. I could barely form coherent words.

He moved his arms behind my knees, pinning my legs back so he could deepen the angle.

"Oh god…"

"Tell me."

"No…I don't want you to wear a condom."

He gave me a look of satisfaction before he rocked into me at a regular pace, rewarding me with long and even strokes. Quiet moans escaped his lips as he moved in and out. He didn't kiss me, his eyes focused on mine the entire time.

My tits shook every time he rocked into me, and I felt myself tighten around him. An orgasm was bubbling on the horizon. I could feel it slowly approaching, like when the sun set over the edge of the Earth just before dark.

"Fuck…" He pressed his head to mine as he worked his

ass and hips to pound his dick inside my pussy. "Sweetheart..."

My hands moved up his chest, and my fingers snaked into his hair, feeling the damp sweat collect over the back of his neck. I took his length balls deep every single time, and I loved feeling his sac smack against my ass.

He pulled away and looked me in the eyes again. "I love you."

I stopped breathing when I heard the words, floored by the confession I hadn't heard him make until now. He told me he wanted to be with me, to grow old with me, but he never said those words to me like that before.

"I miss this..." He kissed my forehead before he rested his head against mine.

I was already on the verge of a powerful climax, and he pushed me over the edge. I plummeted down violently, the spasms of pleasure vibrating through my body. "Cypress... god." I yelled in his face, unable to keep my voice down and under control. My slickness increased in waves and soaked his cock.

"Mmm..." He closed his eyes as he enjoyed me, probably feeling the way my body reacted to his. He positioned himself farther over me, deepening the angle so he could get every inch inside me.

I grabbed his ass and pulled him harder into me, knowing he was just about to come. My nipples were hard as daggers, and my body was warm, ready to feel that mound of come sit deep inside me.

He came with a moan and filled me, his breathing rough and ragged. He wrapped his arm around me and pulled me tighter against him as he pinned me against the mattress, making sure not a single drop was spilled. He wanted to give me everything he had.

And I wanted to take it just as much.

He remained glued to me as he caught his breath, his cock still inside me and his come mixed with mine. Slowly, he began to soften, and the pressure inside my channel decreased. He pulled away and looked me in the eye, his body flushed with heat and redness from the pounding blood. "I'm not finished with you."

WE SPENT THE REST OF THE DAY IN BED, SWITCHING FROM making love to talking during the breaks in between. Cypress placed a bottle of wine on the nightstand along with two glasses. We sipped it as we enjoyed each other's company and that of Dino, who'd followed Cypress when he came back with the wine.

I tried not to think about what I was doing. Whenever I did that, I felt guilty for my actions. But sometimes over-thinking it was the worst thing you could. Just living in the moment and going with it were often the best approaches.

Cypress had himself propped on one elbow as he drank his wine and watched me.

I stared back, feeling his gaze roam over every feature on my face. He could stare for hours and hardly blink. It was a look he hadn't given me the first time we were together. It was a new trait he must have picked up after we got married.

I eyed his clock on the nightstand. "It's getting late."

"Yeah. I'm old and barely stay up past ten anymore."

"Me too. But I like being up early. It's nice when you have the whole day ahead of you."

"True."

I'd spent the whole day having sex with him, and I wasn't sure if I could get out of the bed without spilling his seed everywhere. He stuffed me as much as he could, and I knew it was on purpose. I hoped I could make it to the bathroom without getting it everywhere. "I should get going..."

He grabbed my wrist and kept me in place. "Why should you get going?"

"I should shower and go to bed. We both established we're old and need our beauty rest."

"I have a king-size bed right here." He set down his wine then placed his palm over his chest. "And a personal heater here. You've got everything you need."

"You know the hospitality isn't the problem..."

He turned more aggressive. "Sweetheart, stay."

"Cypress, I shouldn't..."

"Why?" he demanded. "You're the one who asked me to hang out. We spent all day making love. Give me one good reason why you should leave when I'm asking you to stay."

"Because I don't want to rush anything. I told you our physical relationship was meaningless."

"It's not meaningless, and we both know it. Now sleep with me. Don't fuck me and then leave. I'm asking you to stay."

I searched his eyes, seeing the sincerity that was borderline desperate. "Why is it so important to you?"

He loosened his grip on my wrist when he realized I wasn't going to slip away. "I slept beside you every night for months. When you left... I've never been able to sleep the same since. It'll be nice to feel you beside me again, even if it's just for a night."

Now if I left I would feel like a terrible human being. Cypress was two different people in my eyes at the same time. He was sweet and loyal, the kind of partner that would never hurt me. At other times, he was the guy who broke my heart and would do it again. Right now, he was that first guy. "Okay."

He got comfortable beside me and wrapped his arms around my body, hugging me against him. His masculine smell washed over me, hinting of pine needles and body wash. He pulled my leg over his hip and rested his hand against the skin between my shoulder blades.

Now I wanted to stay there forever. Getting my memory back and realizing my life had passed me by and I'd missed so much of it disturbed me. It was terrifying seeing that my nieces had grown so much, my business had changed, and my sister was dealing with a divorce I never knew happened. But Cypress made me feel better about all of that because he was the one thing I could rely on. He was always next door to me, and he was always patient, telling me about everything I missed and explaining it in such detail that I got to experience it.

Sometimes his cheating seemed irrelevant when I thought about all the other sacrifices he'd made.

Like taking care of me every day even though I hated him the whole time. Well, except the times he got me into bed.

His phone rang on his nightstand, vibrating loudly.

Cypress sighed against me, refusing to move.

"Are you gonna get that?"

"Couldn't care less who it is."

The phone went silent.

I closed my eyes and felt Dino move at the end of the bed, repositioning himself so he could get comfortable. Cypress's regular breathing acted as a hypnotic sound, making my mind slowly drift away.

Then his phone rang again.

Now I wondered who was calling him. Was it a woman looking for a booty call?

Cypress sighed then turned over. He snatched the phone, looked at the screen, and then ignored the call before he set it on the nightstand again. He turned back to me and got comfortable.

He obviously had no intention of telling me who was calling him at nine in the evening, and my curiosity was getting the best of me. What if it was a woman? Maybe he had hooked up with someone, and tonight she was calling to see if he was interested in another round. Now I couldn't go to sleep because I couldn't stop thinking about it. I was jealous and hurt over a phone call I knew nothing about.

Was this how I would always feel?

Would I always be this paranoid? This insecure? This jealous? I didn't like it at all. It wasn't who I was as a person.

Cypress must have felt the tension because he opened his eyes and looked at me. "What?"

If I didn't get to the bottom of it, I would always wonder. I needed to know who it was that was calling him this late. "Who was that?"

"Blade."

"If it was him, why didn't you answer?'"

He raised an eyebrow. "Because I'm with you."

It didn't seem like he was lying, but in the back of my mind, I wondered if he was.

Cypress sighed before he grabbed the phone off the nightstand then showed me the call list. "See?" He scrolled through the entire thing, showing me all the people he'd been in contact with recently.

I felt terrible.

He opened his text messages and did the same thing.

The only correspondence he had was with the gang and a few other guys I didn't recognize.

I didn't like this at all.

"I have nothing to hide, sweetheart." He set his phone on his nightstand. "Go through my phone all you want. Doesn't bother me one bit."

But I didn't want to go through his phone. I didn't want to be this person. I wanted the paranoia and suspicions to go away. I wanted to be the easygoing person I once was, not this psycho, jealous person. "I don't want to be that person. I don't like who I turn into anytime a woman walks by or your phone lights up."

"Then trust me."

"I can't do that either." I kicked the covers back and got out of bed.

Cypress didn't fight me this time.

I got dressed with my back turned to him, not wanting to see his look of disappointment after I'd already agreed to sleep there. Now I wanted to leave, to think about what I was really getting myself into.

Cypress got dressed without uttering a single protest, knowing he was going to walk me to the door and say goodnight.

That walk across the house was awkward.

We arrived at his front door and barely made eye contact with each other. There was nothing Cypress could say that hadn't already been said. And I didn't have anything to say either. I wished I could forget what he did and hop back into bed with him, but something always came up. "I'll see you tomorrow."

"Yeah." It was the first time he'd actually seemed mad at me. He wasn't affectionate or gentle like he had been just a few minutes ago. The resentment washed over me like the ocean tide, cold and powerful. "See you tomorrow."

I walked out and didn't expect a hug or kiss goodbye. I went down the steps and heard his front door shut. Normally, he'd wait until I was in my house or walk me to the doorstep. But he didn't do either of those things this time.

This time, he gave up.

"IS IT TOO LATE TO CALL?"

Amelia sighed into the phone. "Bree, you know there's no such thing as too late when it comes to me. What's up?"

"Are the girls asleep?"

"Yeah. They were pooped out today. We went shopping, had lunch, and then went to the beach."

"That sounds nice. Was Ace with you?"

"No. Why?"

"No reason...just curious."

"So, what's up?" she asked.

"Well...I spent the day with Cypress."

"That sounds nice. How'd that go?"

"It went pretty well until this pretty woman started talking to him at the beach. I got so jealous and upset. He told me she'd made a pass at him before, and I can't stop wondering if he hooked up with her. He said he didn't, but I can't get myself to trust him. And then Blade called him when we were in bed together, and I had a hard time believing that too. He had to show me his phone to give me peace of mind."

Amelia took all of it in, listening attentively. "It'll take time to trust him again. No one blames you for being uneasy about it. I know it's hard to believe, but Ace, Blade, and I didn't listen to anything he said for a long time. We were just as distrustful as you are right now."

"I know, but...I don't like what he's turned me into."

"I don't catch your meaning."

"Like, I don't want to be that woman who has to check his phone all the time. I don't want to accuse him of lying every time he says something to me. It turns me into this person I despise. I used to be so much more relaxed and chill. And now...I feel like a bitch. I don't like Cypress because he makes me this way. I know I'm not making sense..."

"No, I totally understand," she whispered. "I just hope I'm not like that when the next guy comes around, paranoid and insecure. After the way Evan left me, I wouldn't be surprised if it happened. We've been scarred by men, and that's hard to erase."

"But I don't feel that way about all men. If I started dating someone else, I wouldn't think twice about that. But with Cypress...he made a fool out of me. I never thought he would hook up with his ex again. I planned a birthday party for him while he was screwing her. I just feel so embarrassed."

"Bree, don't be embarrassed. No one thought less of you for that. We just hated him."

"Bottom line is, I don't like what he turns me into. There are times when I think we could make it work. He's sweet, loyal, funny, and super sexy. I love it when he smiles. I love it when he holds me. But...this stuff always comes back to haunt us. Every single time we're together, it happens. And I suspect that's never going to change."

"It will—"

"I don't think so. And I don't want to be in a relationship

with him if that's how I'm going to be all the time—spying on him. That's not a relationship."

"I agree. Which is why I keep telling you to take your time. You'll trust him again. Just be patient."

"I don't know, Amy..."

"You will. I've seen it happen with my own eyes. Remember that."

I was skeptical. I knew myself pretty well, and I didn't think this was going to change. I cared about Cypress a lot, as much as I hated to admit it. He'd become a friend to me —something more than that. I didn't want to treat him this way, to make him feel like an asshole every single day of our lives. "I love Cypress. And I think that's why we need to go our separate ways."

"Bree, hold on—"

"He doesn't deserve to be insulted every single day. He made a mistake, and I believe he's sorry about it. I believe he's a good guy. But I'm never going to get over this. He deserves to have a clean slate with someone else, just as I deserve to have the same thing with someone else."

"You're just upset right now. Sleep on it—"

"Do I sound upset?" I asked calmly. "I'm just being logical here. We're trying to make this work because we're already married. If we weren't, this wouldn't be happening. We're just forcing it."

"You're forgetting that you guys made it work the first time. You're forgetting that you fell in love with him and you were the happiest I'd ever seen you."

"Well...something must have been different then because that's not how I feel now."

"Cypress isn't going to accept that. He'll keep fighting for you."

"I think after we talk, he'll change his mind."

She sighed. "Trust me, he won't."

"We've been doing this for two months, and it's not working. I'm pulling the plug."

"Bree, listen to me. I'm your sister, and I only want the best for you. I really think Cypress is the best for you."

There was no doubt that I loved spending time with him. There was no doubt I was attracted to him. That I cared about him. "Maybe one day. But not right now. I need to see Cypress the way you guys do. That's not gonna happen if he's constantly seducing me and manipulating me. It has to be natural. And right now, it's not."

Amelia finally went quiet when she realized nothing would change my mind.

"I'm sorry. I know you guys all wanted this to work, but it's not working. I think this is the best thing for Cypress too, even if he doesn't see it right now."

Amelia still didn't say anything.

"Amy?"

"I'm here," she whispered.

"Don't be mad at me."

"I'm not," she said quickly. "I know I have to respect how you feel. When you wanted to get back together with him the first time, I told you to forget about him and he wasn't good enough for you. I warned you he would hurt you again. Obviously, he proved me wrong. But I know how I felt at the time...so I can't hold this against you."

"Thank you." I was glad someone finally understood where I was coming from. They all had these memories of Cypress, memories I couldn't acquire no matter how many stories I heard. It had to be this way, and there was no way around it.

THE NEXT MORNING, I WALKED BACK TO HIS FRONT DOOR AND knocked. His windows were closed today, so I assumed he was pissed and wanted his privacy. But this conversation needed to happen.

He opened the door in just his sweatpants. He was the sexiest on lazy weekends, when he forgot about the shirt and left his chest bare. His hair was messy because he hadn't showered, but that looked good too. "What's up?" He wasn't warm like he usually was. In fact, he was pretty damn cold.

"Can I come in? I want to talk to you."

He opened the door wider and walked to the kitchen table. He plopped down with a clenched jaw, like he already anticipated what I was going to say.

I sat across from him and tried to ignore his obvious hostility. Maybe he would accept my decision because he was so fed up with me. It would certainly make things easier. "I've been doing some thinking, and I don't think this is going to work. I'm never gonna get past my insecurities and trust issues. I wish I could, but I can't. And it's not fair to you, Cypress. I hate being this cold and shrill person when I know that's not who I really am."

He stared out the window, his fingers resting on the table.

I expected more of a reaction than that. "You deserve better. I deserve better. I think we should get a divorce and be friends. Maybe, in time, things will change, but they aren't going to change when it's being forced."

Still, nothing.

"Cypress?"

He slowly turned his head my way, the look in his eyes maniacal. "What do you expect me to say?"

"I just...I want you to understand."

"Well, I'm not an idiot, and I can understand English pretty well," he snapped.

"You know that's not what I meant."

"I don't give a shit what you meant."

I wasn't gonna put up with that tone. "Excuse me?"

He straightened in his chair and leaned forward, looking like a monster rather than a man. "I've been through hell for the past two years. I've had to put up with your memory impairment every single goddamn day. I've paid your bills, made sure you were safe, took care of your business, and took care of your sister when she was losing her sanity. I did all of that—for you. This is how you repay me?" He threw his arms up. "The doctors told me you were never going to get better. Our friends said you weren't going to get better, and I should move on. But did I do that? No. Because I promised to love you no matter what, and I kept my word. When it's your turn to uphold the promise, you turn your back. That's unacceptable to me. Yes, I cheated on you one time with a woman I don't even care about, but when it really mattered, I was there." He slammed his fist on the table. "I was there every fucking day. I get that you can't remember anything that happened, but you did marry me. You did promise to love me for the rest of your life. You should trust your instructs and give this a real effort. From day one, you've never really tried."

I felt the tears burn in my eyes, preparing to drip down my face.

"Get over it, Bree." He slammed his fist down again. "I fucked up one time three years ago. But ever since then, I've been the best damn husband in the world. You wanna get divorced and call it quits? Fine by me. I'm sick of this bull-shit." He grabbed the table and flipped it over, making it clatter on the stone floor. "Get out."

The table didn't touch me as it fell to the ground. It lay at my feet, the vase that had been sitting on top shattered to pieces. His back was to me, so I finally let the tears stream down my cheeks. Before he could see my face, I walked out of his house and slammed the door behind me.

I felt sick.

I felt hurt.

And I felt lost.

4

When I walked in, Ace and Blade were already there.

"What's up?" Blade asked. "How was your weekend?"

"Good. The girls and I hung low," I answered. "What about you?"

"Nothing," Blade said.

"Morning," Ace said, looking sexy in his t-shirt. Even when he didn't say much, his presence was calming. There was nowhere else in the world I'd rather be than by his side.

I sat at my desk and tried not to stare at him. Anytime we were in the same room together, it got my blood going. "Morning. What are the zones?"

Cypress burst through the door and nearly dented the wall because he swung it so hard. Without saying a word, he told everyone he was psychotically pissed, and it would be stupid to mess with him that morning. "I'll take care of Amelia's Place." He unzipped his jacket and hung it on the back of the chair. "Anything before I go?"

Blade eyed Ace, silently asking him what we should do.

Ace shrugged in response.

I took the reins. "Everything alright, Cypress?"

"Definitely." He walked back to the door. "Bree and I are getting a divorce, and I'm moving on with my life. Couldn't be fucking happier." He slammed the door even harder on his way out, making the whole floor shake with the force.

"What did he just say?" Blade asked.

"Divorce?" Ace asked.

So Bree actually went through with it. "Bree mentioned this to me a few nights ago. I figured Cypress would have talked her out of it..."

"No, it looks like she just pissed him off instead," Blade said. "I don't think I've ever seen him that angry."

"Me neither," Ace said.

"What do we do?" Blade said.

"I don't think there's anything we can do," I whispered. "I tried to talk Bree out of it, but she wouldn't listen to me."

"Jesus." Blade rubbed his temple. "I suspect we're gonna be hearing a lot of yelling and screaming for the next few weeks."

"We should invest in a pair of earplugs," Ace said.

I wished Bree hadn't done this. I understood the way she felt, but I really did believe Cypress was the best guy for her.

A minute later, Bree walked inside. She wasn't angry like Cypress. In fact, she was completely the opposite. With a pale face and sad lips, she took a seat at her desk without looking at any of us. "I know what you guys are gonna say, and I really don't want to talk about it right now."

"No problem," Ace said. "You know we're here if you need us."

"Yeah," Blade added.

Bree nodded and stared at her laptop, closing off from us.

I suspected she would talk to me but not in front of

everyone else. That would have to wait until later. "Well, I should get to work."

"Me too," Blade said. "Let's go."

Ace got out of his chair and walked with us to the door.

Bree remained at her desk, and it didn't seem like she was going to move.

"You gonna be okay, Bree?" I asked.

"Yeah," she whispered. "I just need a few minutes."

I shut the door and walked downstairs with the guys. Instead of going to work like they said, they walked into the diner, which hadn't opened just yet. "What are you guys doing?"

"Talking to Cypress," Blade said. "I have to know what happened."

"Me too," Ace said.

Cypress was standing at the counter getting the register ready for the morning. When he looked at us, he still had that ferocious gleam in his eyes. "What?"

Ace leaned against the counter. "Bree just came into the office. Seems pretty down."

"Yeah." Blade rested his arms on the wood. "Thought you might want to talk about it."

"I'm on your side as much as hers," I added, not wanting him to think I would turn on him now that my sister wanted nothing to do with him.

Cypress unrolled the cash and put it in the register. "There's not much to share. She asked for a divorce, and I'm giving it to her." He wasn't wearing his wedding ring like he usually did either. It was weird to see him without it.

"Then why are you so angry?" Blade asked.

Cypress slammed the drawer shut. The workers in the kitchen were stacking plates and firing up the grill, getting ready to serve breakfast to the customers that would show up the second the doors were open. "Because I was there for her when the shit hit the fan. I was there for her when she needed me most. I didn't turn my back on her." He looked at me. "I took care of you when you went through the biggest depression of your life." He turned back to the guys. "Most people wouldn't have stuck it out. Most guys would have moved on and gotten remarried by now. But I didn't do that. I stayed. And she can't give me a chance? She can't keep her own promise—after everything I did for her? I cheated on her one time, I didn't try to murder her. I'm sick of being patient with her. The first time around, it wasn't this bad. She's too stubborn, and frankly, too selfish. It's not gonna work, and I'm not gonna waste my time anymore."

My heart broke as I listened to Cypress. I knew he was angry right now, but underneath that rage, he was devastated. When Bree got her memory back, he was happy to the point of tears. But now his resolve had waned. He'd given up. "Cypress, I know you're upset right now—"

"We spent the day together on Saturday," he continued. "We went to the beach, had some lunch...it wasn't perfect. She got jealous a few times, and the past came up. Whatever. I'm okay with those bumps. I'm okay with her fears. Then we ended up in bed together for most of the day, making love and talking...and then she leaves me. She walks out, and the next day she says she wants a divorce." He stared at the register and shook his head. "I can't keep getting hurt like this. She's not the only one going through a hard time. The world doesn't revolve around her."

Blade nodded in understand. "I'm sorry, man..."

"Me too," Ace said. "I wish there were something we could do."

Cypress shook his head. "I wish there were something you could do too."

"What are you going to do, then?" I asked.

"I'm putting the house back on the market," Cypress said. "I'm getting a divorce. And I'm gonna move on with my life. Maybe in a few years, I can fall in love again and start a family. But right now, I'm just focusing on the house and the divorce."

I couldn't believe this was happening. I knew Bree and Cypress would struggle, but I believed they would make it work in the end. Looked like I was wrong. "We're here if you need anything."

"Yeah," Blade whispered.

"Always," Ace said.

"I know," Cypress whispered.

"Maybe you should take the day off," Ace said. "If you don't want to be next door to Bree, you could always crash at my place. Not a big deal."

"Yeah, maybe you should go home," Blade said. "We can manage without you."

Cypress hesitated, like he was really thinking about it. But then he picked up the wad of cash again and returned to setting up the register. "No. I've gotta move on. And this is the beginning of that."

ACE CAME INTO AMELIA'S PLACE FOR LUNCH. I WAS SITTING AT the counter on my break, and he took the seat beside me. One of the waitresses came over and took his order before she walked away.

"How's it going?" I asked.

He pulled out his phone and set it on the counter. "Good. I'm starving." He peeked over his shoulder and saw Cypress still busy at the counter, ringing up customers and taking them to their seats. "How's he been?"

I took a bite of my turkey sandwich then wiped my lips with a napkin. "He's kept to himself all morning. Not in the mood to talk."

"Hope he's not screaming at the customers."

"No, he's put on a pretty good front."

"Have you talked to Bree?"

"No. I'm gonna swing by the café when I'm off and have a little talk with her." I didn't want my sister to make the biggest mistake of her life, and I had to try to talk some sense into her one more time.

"I wish you the best of luck."

"Thanks."

The waitress set his food in front of him, and Ace immediately began to eat. "Heard from Evan?"

"Not since that one day."

"I hope it wasn't a fluke."

I hoped the same thing. I'd be even more devastated if I didn't hear from him again. "I told him the girls love spending time with him and I'd like it if we could be friends. I was really nice to him, nicer than I should have been. I made sure he felt welcomed as much as possible. So I don't think that was a one-time thing."

"Hope you're right." He took another bite of his sandwich, and his phone lit up with a message from Lady.

I purposely looked at the clock, not wanting to read what she had to say. I was definitely jealous of her. She got to sleep in Ace's bed whenever she wanted. She got to have him in a way I never could, even if they weren't serious.

Ace locked his phone and didn't respond to what she said. "If Evan is difficult, I can handle it."

"That won't be necessary. I want us to be parents

together. I don't want him to be there because he feels obligated."

Ace nodded. "It's gonna be weird working with Cypress and Bree without them being together."

"We don't know that," I said. "Things can change."

He took another bite then wiped his fingers on his napkin. "I've never seen Cypress ever give up. The fact that he says he's gonna get the divorce tells me it's really over... even if Bree wanted to make it work."

That was my worst fear, and Ace just confirmed it. I'd never seen Cypress let the struggle get him down. But now, he was officially defeated. He'd thrown in the towel, and he was concentrating on the future. It probably was over. "I wish it didn't turn out this way."

"Me too. I just hope they can learn to be friends and get along for the business. Because if one of them leaves, it'll really make things messy for all of us."

"True." I hadn't thought of that. Hopefully, it wouldn't come to that.

Ace checked the time on his watch. "I should get going. I barely had time to eat, but the restaurant was packed."

"Then why did you waste time coming down here?" I popped a fry into my mouth.

He shrugged as he got out of the swivel chair. "I was craving a sandwich." He slipped his phone into his pocket then adjusted the sleeves of his collared shirt. Even when he was fully dressed, his beautiful physique was obvious to anyone who wasn't blind. "I'll see you later."

"Bye." I stared at his ass when he turned around and walked away. I remembered the last time he slept over and the vicious way I grabbed his ass and pulled him into me when he came. If I could have that every night, I'd be a happy woman.

I CALLED ACE WHEN I WAS OFF WORK.

He answered on the first ring. "Hey. What's up?"

"I'm going to talk to Bree right now. I hate to ask but—"

"I'll pick up the girls. Don't worry about it."

He was an angel on earth. "Thank you so much."

"No problem. I'll take them to the Rio Grill for a snack."

"Thanks. I appreciate it."

"Just buy me a beer or something."

I chuckled. "I'll buy you a whole case. How about that?"

"Sounds good."

I got off the phone and walked into the café. Bree was behind the register, looking as miserable as she did earlier that morning. The place had just closed, and she was finishing clearing the tables and closing up the café.

Most of her employees were already gone, so we had some privacy when I walked up to the register. "Hey."

She looked up, and it was one of the few times in our lives when she was disappointed to see me. "Hey...I said I didn't want to talk about it right now. Maybe tomorrow."

"You don't have until tomorrow, Bree."

"Sorry?" Her hair was pulled back into a tight ponytail, and I could tell she hadn't taken a shower that morning. She didn't put on any makeup either, and I could see the bags under her eyes. She obviously didn't get much sleep.

"I understand the way you feel. Really, I do. But honestly...Cypress is right about everything."

She stared at me with no reaction.

"I never want to influence your decisions, but I think you're going to regret this. I know what Cypress did was wrong, but he's so much more than that. He really did do everything he could to take care of you. Maybe he wasn't loyal to you before, but he's certainly committed to you now. You honestly can't disagree with that."

She lowered her gaze before she nodded. "I know..."

"I've never seen Cypress this angry before. He said he wants to move on with his life. He said he wants to fall in love again and start a family. You need to do something today. Not tomorrow. Tell him you've changed your mind before he won't change his."

Bree took a deep breath before her eyes watered. "When he told me how he felt...I understood where he was coming from. I knew he was right. But I'm also right, you know?"

"Yeah, I do," I whispered.

"I wish it weren't so complicated..."

"Love is always complicated, Bree."

"I wish I could get over it like the rest of you, but—"

"Cypress never pressured you to get over it. He just asked for you to make things work. You never did that. You always had one foot in and one foot out."

She nodded in agreement.

"Please go talk to him. Make this work while you still have a chance. He's still at Amelia's Place. I think he's going to Ace's afterward."

She nodded again.

"I know you're never gonna find a guy better than Cypress. He's the most loving and loyal man I know. I would never tell you to be with someone unless I truly thought he was right for you."

"I know, sis..."

"So, you'll talk to him?"

"Yeah, I will. If he really did all that stuff for me, I guess I owe it to him. I owe it to myself, considering I decided to marry him to begin with."

I nodded.

"I just hope it's not too late. I've never seen him that angry."

I wanted to tell her it wasn't too late, but I really didn't know this time. "Let's hope he loves you as much as we know he does."

WHEN I CAME HOME, THE GIRLS WERE SITTING AT THE TABLE in the living room working on their homework. Ace was a super parent, getting them to do things that took me twice as long to accomplish. "Thank you so much, Ace." I placed the six-pack of beer on the table. "I owe you one."

"You don't owe me anything." He pulled a bottle out. "But I'll definitely take one of these." He was dressed down in jeans and a gray t-shirt, his body looking particularly fit that day. Or maybe it was just because I hadn't gotten laid in a week.

"How were they?"

"Angels, like always. We got a snack then they got to work. Pretty uneventful. So, did you talk to Bree?"

"Yeah. I did the best I could. She said she would talk to Cypress. I hope things will blow over."

"That makes two of us." He twisted off the cap and took a drink. "They're probably talking right now."

"Yeah, probably."

Ace leaned against the counter and looked into the living room, watching the kids in front of the TV. "You want me to pick up some dinner?"

Did he want to stay and hang out? Because I would love that. "Sure. Or I could cook something."

"You know I never turn down a home-cooked meal. What are you thinking?"

"I was gonna make some pork chops, potatoes, and asparagus."

"That sounds awesome. I'll definitely stick around for that."

I hid my smile as much as I could, not wanting him to know how much his compliments meant to me. "Wanna help?"

"Of course. What can I do?"

"I'll take care of the meat if you handle the potatoes."

"Sure thing." Like we were at work, he took care of his zone, and I took care of mine. My girls stayed in the living room, talking to each other as they worked on their math homework in front of the TV.

For a moment, it reminded me of the way it felt when Evan was still around. But I realized it was never like this. Evan never wanted to help me make dinner; he only did it when I asked. After working all day, he just wanted to sit on the couch and stare at the screen, fading away like I didn't exist.

Before I could let the thought get me down, I thought about the happy moment I was in. I had a great friend who showed me the kind of love I needed at the time. And that was all I needed.

AFTER DINNER WAS FINISHED, I HAD THE GIRLS WASH UP THEN go to bed. They were always asleep by eight thirty, which was way earlier than I ever went to sleep. I returned to the kitchen to see Ace cleaning everything up.

"You don't have to do that, Ace." I took over at the sink and rinsed all the dishes before I let them sit at the bottom.

"I don't mind."

"The dishes can be done tomorrow." I wrapped up the leftovers and put them in the fridge.

"Dinner was great. Thanks for including me."

"Well, thanks for looking after my kids."

"You don't need to thank me for that. They're great." He smiled as he leaned against the counter, looking handsome as hell like always.

I hated Lady even more now. "Well, I guess I'll see you tomorrow." I walked to the entryway then opened the front door. "I suspect we'll find out what happened with Bree and Cypress then."

"Or maybe they both won't show up, and we'll know everything went to shit." He stood beside me in the entryway but didn't walk outside. His eyes were on me, his expression unreadable.

A prickle began at the top of my spine and slowly trickled down. I could feel my muscles tense and coil, imagining how his fingers felt when they dug into my skin. When I rode him, he gripped me with the ferocity with which every man should grab his woman. It was dangerous when we were alone together. We needed witnesses at all times so my mind wouldn't run into the gutter.

I wish we had witnesses now.

Ace continued to stand there, his hands in his pockets.

I didn't know what he was waiting for, but I hoped he was thinking the exact same thing I was thinking. If we had another slipup, I wouldn't be opposed to it. I certainly didn't have the strength to say no when my entire body was saying yes.

Ace's expression darkened further. "I want to make love to you again."

I could feel my pulse throbbing in my neck. My heart

worked harder to carry the adrenaline to the rest of my body. My knees felt weak, and my palms felt sweaty.

"I know I should leave...but I don't want to."

Now all logic slipped from my mind. I knew this was just a booty call that meant nothing to him, but I loved the way he made me feel when we were together. I pressed my palm against the wood and shut the door before I moved into his chest. "Then don't." My arms snaked around his neck, and I pressed my mouth to his, feeling the scorching sensation I only experienced when we were in the same room together.

His arms locked around me just the way I liked, and he kissed me back with the same passion. We stood in the entryway in the darkness, kissing and touching each other with no intention of stopping. The dishes sat in the sink, and the TV was still on in the living room.

Neither one of us cared.

Ace backed me up against the door and kissed me harder, his hands groping every inch of my body. He touched me everywhere, making sure there wasn't a single place that wasn't worshiped by him.

I wanted our clothes to be gone. I wanted it just to be us and our naked bodies against my sheets. We could fuck against the door and I would enjoy it, but I wanted more. Now that we'd screwed enough times, I was perfectly comfortable giving and taking what I wanted. "Bedroom." I ended the kiss and grabbed his hand before I pulled him toward the bedroom. Luckily, my room was on the opposite side of the house from the girls. A quiet creak or a gentle moan wouldn't reach their innocent ears.

We got into my bedroom and yanked our clothes off as fast as we could. We didn't even undress each other, focusing on getting naked as quickly as possible. Once the clothes were gone, he picked me up and held me against his chest. His big hands gripped my ass and thighs, and with strength that was so masculine, he lifted me onto his length and sheathed himself in my pussy.

"Ace..." My arms hooked around his shoulders, and I kissed him as he lifted me up and down, using his powerful arms to move me without any hint of exhaustion. His strength was undeniable, and he made me feel lighter than a feather.

He gave me his tongue as he moved me up again, successfully doing two things at once. I'd never fucked like this before, and I really liked it. I liked the way my tits shook every time he bounced me up and down. His body developed a coating with sweat, and I could feel the moisture under my fingertips. I wanted to cry out in pleasure, feeling so full every time he lowered me onto his length, but I always silenced my voice because we weren't alone.

I wondered what kind of sex we could have if we were.

Ace stopped kissing me and watched my expression as he lifted me up and down. He had the looks of an old-fashioned movie star, so hard and masculine, that he made every other man I met look soft. He cared about my pleasure as much as his own, and that's what made him even sexier.

I knew I was about to come. I was just seconds away, and his massive cock was pushing me closer to the edge. I gripped him tighter, sliced his wet skin with my fingertips, and released a suppressed moan that was volcanic in nature.

He sealed his mouth over mine and silenced my orgasm with his lips, sucking my moans into his throat.

Thank god he was there. Otherwise, I would have woken up both of my kids with my recklessness.

Ace slowed down, moving me up and down and at a gentler pace. His cock thickened inside me, and he released a restrained moan as he filled me, depositing his seed deep inside my pussy.

I loved that feeling, of being full with his length and his come.

Ace carried me to the bed and laid me down on the mattress, his cock still inside me. He sank into the bed with his weight and positioned himself on top of me.

I wasn't sure if he was preparing to leave, but I didn't want him to go. I wanted a passionate night without any sleep. I wanted to feel alive and desirable. I wanted to be exactly the way he saw me, as a beautiful woman he wanted to make love to. "I don't want you to go..." I ran my hands up his chest and locked my ankles together around his back.

He kissed the corner of my mouth before he dug his hand into my hair. "I'm not going anywhere."

5

BLADE

My interaction with the woman from the coffee shop lasted two minutes at most, but I hadn't stopped thinking about her—even days later. I wanted to know if she was from France. And if so, what part? I wanted to know how long she planned on sticking around. I wanted to know if she had a boyfriend.

God, I hoped not.

I walked to the coffee shop in the courtyard and got in line behind the five people already standing there. People chitchatted at the tables, and birds sang from their places along the wall and flowers.

I looked behind the counter discreetly, hoping to see the French babe I hadn't stopped thinking about.

The person working the register was some dude.

Dammit.

I looked at everyone else behind the counter, but I didn't see the pretty brunette who didn't have a name. Maybe she wasn't working today. I would come by every day to check, but that would be way too creepy. Besides, I wasn't that kind of guy. I'd chase a woman for a little while, but I wouldn't overdo it. No woman was worth that much effort. If she liked me, great. If she didn't, whatever.

I moved farther up in the line, and there was still no sight of her.

Damn.

When I finally got to the register, she came out from the back with a tray of slab pie. She walked to the deli window and carefully set every piece on display.

I bet she was as sweet as that pie.

"Hello?" The guy at the register spoke to me in an annoyed tone.

My eyes moved to his. "Huh?"

"Are you gonna order something?"

Why did I always have to look like an idiot when I was standing there. "A black coffee and I'll take one of those pies."

"Got it." He rang me up and took my money.

She noticed that I was standing there, and her eyes landed on me with a slight reaction of familiarity. Her smile widened, showing those perfectly white teeth. Today, she wore skintight denim jeans that rose to her belly button and a short top that showed half an inch of her skin. A loose blouse was on top along with that same gold necklace I saw her wear last time. One side of her hair was pinned back, showing her cheek and slender neck.

She looked even more beautiful than she did the other day.

"Blueberry or apple?"

This time, I was going to say something. I wasn't gonna let my mouth hang open like a dumb moron. "Blueberry, please."

She placed it in a recyclable container and handed it over. "Here you go."

"Thanks." I grazed one of her fingers when I took the container, feeling the jolt of attraction I was already experiencing.

"You're welcome." She turned her gaze down and focused on what she was doing.

I turned around and walked away, holding my coffee and my pie. Before I walked down the stone walkway, I stopped. I could keep coming back here, doing this flirtatious dance, or I could just ask her out and be done with it. I didn't want to beat around the bush for another week. She probably had a boyfriend anyway, so I may as well get my answer now so I could stop thinking about her.

I set my things on an empty table then walked back to the counter, doing my best to appear confident. I walked right up to her, looked her in the eye, and then spoke. "My name is Blade. I was wondering if—"

"Yes."

I lost my footing, not expecting a reaction before I even finished my sentence. "Yes, what?"

"Yes, I'll go out with you. At least...I hope that's what you were asking." A subtle tinge of pink entered her cheeks. "If not, then I'm gonna feel like the biggest dork on the planet, and we should pretend it never happened."

Hearing her call herself a dork suddenly made me like her more. She was gorgeous, but she obviously didn't think that. That French accent made her sound even cuter than she had the first time. "That's definitely what I was asking. Thanks for making it so easy."

That pink color was still in her cheeks, and it was growing steadily, blossoming into red.

"What are you doing tonight?"

"I get off work at five," she said. "After that, my evening is free."

"Can I take you to dinner?"

"Absolutely. How about Little Napoli?"

I liked a woman who took action instead of making me decide everything. "I'll meet you there at seven." I wouldn't offer to pick her up on the first date. Nowadays, women were so terrified of being stalked or harmed that it was a sign of creepiness if I made the offer. It might make it seem like I was trying to figure out where she lived. If she wanted me to know that information, she would tell me. I would never ask.

"Great. See you then."

"I didn't catch your name."

"Celeste."

Definitely French. "I'll see you tonight."

6

Bree

Cypress's words sank into me like a butcher knife. His ferocity and his rage struck a chord, and I felt terrible for hurting someone who obviously loved me. I hated him for what he did to me, but I hated myself more for hurting him.

He made me rethink everything.

Maybe I was wrong.

After I spoke with Amelia, I headed back to the diner where I hoped he still was. The diner hadn't closed just yet, but he may have already taken off. I suspected he wouldn't go back to the house since I was right next door. Even with the shades closed, we were still too close together.

I opened the door to Amelia's Place and walked inside. Cypress was still there, stacking the chairs onto the tables. Maria was putting away clean dishes in the kitchen, so he wasn't alone. I walked inside and stood by the door, unsure what to do next.

Cypress turned around when he heard the door shut. He stiffened when he looked at me, and then he continued working like I didn't exist. His jaw was noticeably tense, and he was just as angry as he had been when he'd screamed at me last night.

"Maria, you can take off," I said. "I'll handle that."

She must have picked up on the tension because she stopped what she was doing and grabbed her purse before she walked out. When she turned the corner and disappeared, we were finally alone together.

Cypress kept working, ignoring me.

"Can we talk?" The sky was overcast, so it wasn't bright in the restaurant. The lights were already turned off in preparation for closing. I placed my hands in my pockets, feeling my heart thump hard against my chest.

He finished the last table, flipping the chairs over and stacking them on top. "There's nothing to talk about." Even though he spoke quietly, his rage was implied in his tone. "We'll get divorced and be business partners. Maybe one day we can friends—but let's not push it." He finished the last chair then crossed his arms over his chest, staying on the far side of the room.

Maybe Amelia was right. I probably was too late. "I thought about everything you said and...you're right. You're right about everything. I've never really given this a chance. I'm still upset about what you did, but I did marry you. So...I should honor that."

He continued to look angry.

"And you've more than proved yourself to me. You've done so much for me and my family."

Still nothing.

"I want to start over, Cypress. I want to work through this together."

"I've been trying to do that for two months," he snapped.

"I know...I know I was difficult."

"Difficult doesn't even begin to describe it."

"I have my insecurities and I will still have them, but I want to make this work. I want to try. Please give me another chance, Cypress."

He dropped his gaze and wouldn't look at me.

"I know you love me…"

He raised his gaze again and looked me in the eye. His anger dimmed, but only slightly.

"Amelia tells me how great we are together. She tells me all the incredible things you've done for me. I just…I didn't appreciate it. I didn't value it. But I do now. If you're the greatest thing that ever happened to me, I don't want to lose you. I can't promise we'll go back to what we were quickly or I'll trust you right away—"

"I never asked for that, Bree. I've always been patient. You can take all the time you need. All I wanted was your commitment."

"Okay…I'll give it to you now."

He sighed under his breath.

Now I really thought he would say no. I'd pushed him too far, and now he was gone. "Cypress, come on…"

He rubbed the back of his neck. "You've hurt me a lot, you know. I'm not a pussy, but sleeping with my wife and then watching her leave me doesn't feel good. Wanting to sleep over and being rejected makes me feel like shit. Putting my heart on the line every day and getting it smashed feels pretty terrible."

"I know…I know that now."

He walked to the window and looked outside, turning his back to me.

I didn't know what else to say. He would either give me another chance, or he wouldn't. I suspected this was the end for us.

He turned back around. "You said you want to give this a real try. How do you intend to do that?"

Did that mean he was giving me another chance? "I don't know. I don't have anything specific in mind. But maybe we can try marriage counseling, have a date night, do sleepovers...stuff like that."

He still looked angry. "I want you to tell me we're going to make this marriage work. There is no possibility of us walking away from each other. I want that off the table for good. This is how it's going to be. No second-guessing. No uncertainty. I can accept things not being perfect and times when you need your space, but I need that. I need us to be husband and wife now."

He was asking for a lot, but he was entitled. He still had been there for me when I completely lost my memory. He could have left me, and no one would have judged him for it. He believed in us when everyone told him there was no hope. "I can do that...if you give me enough time to start trusting you again."

He finally lowered his arms to his sides, the hatred gone from his face. "You have a deal."

———

Cypress had been so livid I didn't expect him to give me another try. But now we walked home together, moving side by side as the sun set over the water. Cypress wore his sweater, and I had my hands stuffed into my pockets.

We didn't speak.

There wasn't anything else to say now that the intense conversation was over, but I didn't know what was waiting for us when we got home. Did we have dinner together? Or should we spend some time apart?

We reached our two houses then stopped at the stone steps.

I thought I should initiate something since I was the one who'd brought us to a boiling point. "You wanna have dinner at my place?"

It was the first time he'd smiled in a few days. "I'd love that."

"Cool." I walked up to the front of the house. "I'll whip something up."

"I smell like food, so I'm gonna shower and change. I'll be over in fifteen minutes with Dino." He walked inside his house and shut the door.

Once I was alone in my house, I finally had a moment to think about what had just happened. I was committed to making this work now. Just the other day, I couldn't picture myself ever giving him a real chance, but something in my gut told me that would be a mistake. I missed his transformation, but I witnessed his changed personality. He wasn't anything like he used to be.

He was definitely different.

I threw together the few items I had in my fridge, making beef stroganoff and asparagus, and he walked inside just before I was finished.

"Something smells good." He joined me at the counter and looked at the stovetop, seeing the meat sizzle in the pan.

"I'm not the best cook, but at least I can guarantee we won't get food poisoning."

"That works for me."

I served the food on the plates then put them on the table. Cypress and I took a seat across from each other, back to saying nothing and pretending our earlier conversation didn't happen—even though we were both thinking about it.

His hair was slightly damp and messy because he'd dried it with a towel. He was dressed down in jeans and a black t-shirt, the muscles of his shoulders and arms looking exquisite. Every time he shifted slightly, the rest of his body rippled like waves in a pond. "It's good. Thanks for making it."

"You're welcome."

Dino made himself comfortable on my couch, using a blanket I'd used to snuggle with the night before. Sometimes a sigh would escape his lips when he took a deep breath and settled in.

I wanted to ask Cypress how his day went, but I already knew that answer. He was pissed off all day long, from the moment he woke up until the moment he finished up his shift. I had been miserable, not eating a single thing because my stomach hurt so much. It was full of stress and acid.

So there was nothing to talk about.

"Anything interesting happen at the café?" he finally asked to break the silence.

"An extra worker showed up today because he thought he had a shift when he didn't. I told him he could stay, but it ended up being slow so I didn't do much other than hang out at the office."

Cypress chuckled. "Money well spent."

"So, do we ever take vacation days? Or do we work all the time?"

"No, we take time off. Amelia takes the most time off because of the girls. We kinda just work around her schedule."

"That's sweet..."

"And when we have kids, I'm sure the gang will pick up the slack for us."

I stilled at the mention of us having children, but I didn't make a comment or overtly react. If I was in this for the long haul, I'd have to accept that possibility. "So, we're off on Saturdays?"

"And Sundays, if you want. But when we aren't there, there's usually more work during the week. So we rotate. One of us will work the weekend and check in on all the restaurants. It's good to be present so the employees always stay honest, you know?"

"People actually steal from us?"

"Not really," he said. "I mean, they do their jobs well. If we aren't around, they might slack off."

"Oh, I see."

He continued eating, shoving large servings of food into his mouth. His jaw shifted as he chewed, his cheeks hollowing out and bringing out his distinct handsomeness. Without looking at me, he spoke. "What are you thinking?"

I didn't respond right away because I hadn't expected him to ask that question. "That you look handsome when you eat. Something to do with your jaw..." Since we were going to make this work, I might as well be as honest as possible.

He grinned as he chewed at the same time. "What a coincidence. I think you look cute all the time."

"Not all the time..." I had bad hair days all the time.

"Nope. All the time."

"Even first thing in the morning?" I asked incredulously.

"Especially." He scraped up every piece of food on his plate until it was nearly as clean as it was when I took it out of the cabinet. "That was pretty damn good."

"I'm glad you liked it. It's one of the few things I can make."

"Shut up, you're a great cook."

"I don't remember that."

"Yeah, you used to cook when we got home every night. I would help you, of course. But you were the one who picked out everything at the store and prepared the meals for the week. I just did what I was told."

"Wow, I'm surprised by that. When did I learn to cook?"

"You picked up things here and there, and you started watching the cooking channel." He rolled his eyes. "You used to be obsessed. We'd watch it every single night."

"Seriously?"

He nodded. "Seriously."

That didn't sound like me at all. "What else did I like to do?"

"You used to read a lot. You got into a Stephen King phase."

"I didn't think I'd like horror."

"He writes fantasy too. I think you preferred that. You also ran your first marathon when we'd been married for four months."

Now I definitely didn't believe that. "Bullshit."

He smiled. "I'm being serious."

"Me? Run a marathon?"

"Yeah, and you did pretty damn good too."

"What made me do that?"

"Blade called you a slug one day, and somehow the two of you made this bet. He said you would never finish, and you had to prove him wrong. And trust me, you proved him wrong."

Once upon a time, I was a great cook and athletic. The version of myself I remembered was lazy and unambitious. "I sound like a different person."

"Because you were. We turned each other into different people...in a good way."

A warmth entered my body, a sensation of goodness I

couldn't explain. It was a small dose of happiness that I hadn't felt in a long time. As if we hadn't just screamed at each other for the past twenty-four hours, the atmosphere felt nice. "Are you still a pig?"

"Excuse me?" he asked, both eyebrows raised.

"Do you still leave your dirty clothes all over the floor? Socks on the couch?"

When he understood what I meant, his smile returned. "No. Living with you was like being stuck in boot camp. If a single sock landed on the floor, you were out for blood. I've continued those practices on my own."

"Looks like marriage served you well."

He chuckled. "It was the best six months of my life. Even now...it's still been the best time of my life." He met my gaze with a soft look, his sincerity obvious.

I softened underneath his gaze, feeling his love pour out and seep into my skin. When we were together the first time, I knew how much I loved him. And I knew how much he loved me—despite what he did.

He reached across the table and rested his hand on mine. His fingertips were warm and heavy, and I remembered exactly how they felt against my nipples when they brushed across my sensitive skin. "This has been hard for both of us...but I'm glad we aren't giving up."

My fingers curled around his. "Yeah...me too."

7

AMELIA

Ace never set his alarm, so we woke up to the sound of my girls fighting in the bathroom.

My eyes cracked open, and panic erupted in my chest. "Shit. Ace." I squeezed his arm.

He sighed then cuddled closer into my side, his thick body getting tangled with mine. "Hmm?"

"We didn't set your alarm, and the girls are awake." I kept whispering so they wouldn't hear me. They were too busy fighting over the Frozen toothpaste to notice anything.

Ace finally opened his eyes then ran his fingers through his hair. "Fuck. Sorry. I forgot."

"It's okay. But what do we do?"

"Take them to school. I'll stay in here until you leave."

"But you won't have time to shower and get ready. Everyone will know something is up."

He wiped the sleep from his eye. "I'll say I stayed at Lady's."

That went down my throat like a stick of dynamite. I didn't care if they knew he slept over. Cypress could get mad

82

E. L. TODD

all he wanted, but I didn't give a damn. I was the one Ace pleased last night, not that woman. "Okay." I didn't say what was on my mind and left the bedroom to get the kids ready for school.

I dropped them off at their school down the road then returned and headed to work. When I walked into the office upstairs, Ace wasn't there yet. He probably went to his place to brush his teeth and fix his hair as much as he could.

I felt like Blade somehow knew what I was doing last night, even though he had no way of knowing. He shook his knee as he stared at me, obviously anxious.

"What's up with you?"

"I just have some news. Was gonna wait until Ace got here."

"I hope it's good."

"It involves a beautiful woman—it's definitely good."

I took a seat at my desk, and after ten minutes passed, Ace walked inside.

"Man, you look terrible," Blade said bluntly. "Did you sleep last night?"

"A little." Ace didn't look at me before he dropped into his chair. He was in slacks and a collared shirt, but his eyes gave away his exhaustion. "What about you?"

"I slept great. But I had an even better morning."

"What happened?" Ace asked.

"There's this French babe at that coffee shop on Ocean and Lincoln. I'd seen her a few times but never had the balls to say anything to her. So I finally asked her out this morning," Blade said. "You know what she said?"

"Get away from me?" Ace teased.

Blade ignored him. "She said yes. I'm taking her to dinner at Little Napoli tonight. I'm excited."

"Good for you, Blade," I said. "I hope it goes well."

"I hope so too," Blade said. "She's super cute."

"How do you know she's French?" Ace asked.

"She has a French accent," Blade explained. "I'll ask her more about it when we have dinner tonight." Blade got out of his chair and pulled his hoodie back on. "I'm hitting the café today. Unless you want me to manage Olives?"

"No, I got it," Ace said. "See you later. Tell me how the date goes."

"I will." Blade walked out.

Now Ace and I were alone together. I wasn't sure what we were going to say to each other. I assumed we were keeping our affair to ourselves. It didn't seem like Ace had any interest in telling the others what we were doing. But now that it had happened so many times, I assumed we had to talk about it.

Ace turned in his chair and looked at me, tired and sexy like he was when I first woke up. "I don't know what's wrong with me."

As vague as the statement was, I knew what he meant.

"I know it's wrong." He rubbed his chin. "I know we should stop. But whenever we're alone together..."

"I know."

He propped his elbow on the desk then ran his fingers through his hair.

"But why do we have to stop?"

He looked up at me, a hint of surprise in his eyes.

"We don't have to tell anyone. We can keep it between us."

"I don't want to make things complicated and ruin our friendship. That's what I'm most concerned about."

"Well, we don't need to worry about that. I can be mature about this. We both can. We've already established it's never going to be anything serious."

"And you're okay with that?" he whispered.

I nodded. "You make me feel like a woman, you know?"

He tilted his head to the side.

"I don't feel like a mom with you. I don't feel like an ex-wife. I just feel like a desirable woman with a hot guy who wants me."

A smile stretched across his lips.

"It's been so long since I've been with anyone, and I like being touched, being kissed, being held...it feels so nice. Even if it doesn't mean anything, just having someone is great. I like sleeping with you. I like being with you." Ace probably wouldn't understand any of that because he was with different women all the time, but I pretty much lived in solitude. "It's my escape. It's the time I can be something else...someone else."

"Amelia, you're a gorgeous woman who could go pick up any guy you wanted at a bar. You could have something meaningful, go on dates and find the right guy. You don't have to settle for me."

"Settle?" I asked incredulously. "Ace, it's not settling. You're the sexiest guy in the world. I love your body. I love the way you kiss me..." A blush moved into my cheeks when I began to share too much. "And you're so sweet. There is no one better than you."

He straightened in his chair and looked at me harder. "I want to say no, that we should just be friends, but I feel like it's gonna happen again anyway."

"And I want it to happen."

His eyes narrowed as if he wanted to cross the room and kiss me then and there, fucking me on the desk and not giving a damn if someone walked in.

Like I'd say no to that.

The door opened and cut through the tension between

us. Cypress and Bree walked inside, and judging from the brightness in their eyes, they weren't at war with each other anymore. "What's up?" Cypress asked. "Did we interrupt something?"

"No," I said quickly, feeling paranoid. "Looks like you two worked things out?"

Bree nodded. "Yeah, we did."

Cypress stood close to her, his arm touching hers. "We're gonna give this another try—and do a better job."

That made me happier than I could let on. I wanted my sister to get back together with Cypress. I wanted things to be back to what they were, when they were both so happy that everyone around them wanted to throw up. "I'm glad to hear that."

"Me too," Ace said. "It's hard to picture you guys ever being with other people."

Cypress grabbed Bree's hand and interlocked their fingers. "No other people. It's just the two of us."

When I saw the way Cypress was with my sister, it gave me hope that true love existed. Evan left me for a superficial reason, but when Bree lost her memory, Cypress never turned his back on her. He was there for her—no matter what. My eyes drifted to Ace, and I knew he would be the exact same way when he found the woman he loved. It would never be me, but I was okay with that. I could enjoy him for now until it was time for him to move on.

And I was still grateful for that.

I HADN'T HEARD FROM EVAN IN A WHILE, SO I GRABBED MY phone and texted him while the girls watched TV in the living room. *Hey. Maybe the four of us could get dinner tomorrow night.* Evan and I hadn't spent any time together, but I wanted us to be a family. I didn't see why the four of us couldn't go out. He could bring his girlfriend if he really wanted to. I wouldn't object as long as he was spending time with our kids.

No response.

It was only seven in the evening, so I didn't think it was too late. But maybe it was.

I put my phone down and spent time with the girls before I put them to bed. They always tried to stay up late, even when their eyelids were heavy and they were falling asleep in front of the TV. I put them to bed before I went in my own bedroom, grateful for the silence I didn't enjoy too often. I thought about texting Ace. Now that we'd accepted our physical relationship, I didn't think it was out of line for me to text him if I wanted to.

But I didn't want to seem too forward. And if he were with Lady, I would just feel uncomfortable.

My phone lit up with a text message from Evan, but it definitely wasn't him.

Don't text my man. He left you for me, and you need to get over it.

My eyes nearly popped out of my head when I read the message. I had to read it a few more times before I finally accepted what I was really looking at. *I was asking the father of my children to spend time with his kids—you get over it.* Two can play that game.

I mean it, bitch.

Whoa, she was psycho. She took the conversation to a whole new place, and I wasn't going to stoop to her level. When she went low, I would go high. *Have a good night. Tell Evan I said hi.*

She didn't say anything back.

I HELPED OUT AT OLIVES THAT AFTERNOON, WHICH WAS NICE because Ace was usually there. I waited on tables while he kept an eye on the restaurant, running food and taking care of tabs when the waitresses were too busy.

I caught him looking at me a few times.

The hours went by, and by late afternoon, we finally finished the lunch shift. I hung up my apron and stuck my tips in my back pocket.

"What are you doing now?" Ace came up behind me, his arm moving past my waist.

My heart hammered. "Picking up the girls then making them a snack. What are you doing?"

"I'm meeting Blade for drinks. He wants to tell me how his date went."

"Oh, I wish I could go. I'd love to hear about it too."

"Why don't you?" he asked.

"Uh, I have two little girls. That's why." I didn't have the social life the others did. Sometimes I didn't think they understood that.

"What's Sara up to?"

"I guess I could see if she's free tonight. I'll let you know."

"Great." He smiled. "I'd love for you to be there."

"Really?" I whispered.

"Yeah. Always." We were in the back office, so his arm circled my waist and he gave me a kiss on the lips.

God, that was nice. My arms immediately circled his waist, and I pressed myself farther into him, needing that hard body against mine. He woke up my body from a deep hibernation, making me feel more alive than I'd been in a long time.

When he pulled away, it didn't seem like he wanted it to end.

Neither did I. "You wanna come over later?" I didn't know if he already had plans with Lady or someone else, but if I reserved him first, I might get him for the night. I pressed my lips tightly together as I waited.

"Yeah." He kissed the corner of my mouth. "I'll be there."

My stomach clenched as it tied up in knots. He made me feel weak and lightheaded every time he kissed me. "Okay..."

He walked out first, and then I followed. I headed in the opposite direction toward my house and pulled out my phone to check my messages. I didn't have my cell phone on me when I was working because it was too distracting. If the school needed to call me about Rose or Lily, they knew how to get ahold of me.

I had a few messages from Evan. And I knew it was the real Evan, not his psycho whore. *Can we talk?*

There were a few other messages from him. *I'm gonna swing by after work. Hope to see you then.*

I wondered what he wanted to talk about. Maybe he saw the messages his girlfriend left. Unless she erased them, there was no way he could miss them. I walked to my house and found Evan's BMW parked in the driveway. He leaned against the passenger door in his slacks and collared shirt with his sunglasses on. He was texting on his phone, so he didn't see me walk up.

"Hey."

He looked up then shoved his phone into his pocket. "Hey. Just got off work?"

"Yeah. I didn't see your messages until now. Everything alright?"

"Uh, yeah." He rubbed the back of his neck, the uncertainty stretching across his face. "Actually, no. I know this is a weird question but...did Rebecca text you from my phone last night?"

So she must have deleted the messages. What a psycho. "Why?"

"I noticed my phone wasn't where I left it, and I know she's looked through it before...and our entire conversation had been deleted."

I admitted she was hot, but why was he seeing her if she was this crazy? "Actually, yeah. I asked if you wanted to get dinner with the girls and me last night." I pulled out my phone and pulled up the conversation. "And this is what she said." I thought it was better if he read the messages himself.

He rubbed his chin as he scrolled through them. "Jesus..." He kept scrolling until he got to the very end. "God, I'm so sorry, Amelia. She's really insecure sometimes. She's always been kinda jealous of you."

"Me?" I asked incredulously. "You left me for her. Why would she be jealous?" She was ten years younger than me and ten times fitter. I was a single mom with two kids. There was no competition.

He winced at my comment. "I'm not sure why she's like that."

It made me wonder if my hunch had been right. That Evan hadn't been spending time with the girls because Rebecca didn't want him to. I'd judge Evan even more harshly if that were the case. "You should tell her to get over it. Whether she likes it or not, you and I are gonna be in each other's lives forever. We have two daughters."

"I know..."

I wouldn't baby this woman, and neither should he. The fact that she acted this way made me concerned. I didn't think I'd ever feel comfortable with her being alone with my girls, not if she was this insecure. And it was even more insulting that Evan left me for a woman who lacked class. He really preferred to be with someone that rude over me? Was I that terrible? Before I could think about it any further and pull myself into another bout of depression, I shook it off. "Well, I should pick up the girls. I'll see you around, Evan."

"Could I come along?"

I wanted to make a jab and ask if that would be okay with this girlfriend, but I chose the high road. "Yeah, sure."

WE DROVE DOWN DOLORES AND PAST MISSION RANCH UNTIL we reached the elementary school. Their play area overlooked the ocean and Point Lobos, and I couldn't believe children had such a spectacular view during the school day.

I parked the car, and Evan and I walked onto the school grounds where the children waited for their parents after the bell rang. School hadn't been dismissed yet, so it was just a group of parents waiting in the courtyard.

Evan and I stood together, not having anything to say.

My phone vibrated in my pocket, so I pulled it out and looked at the screen. I had a message from Ace. *I shouldn't have kissed you at work. Now it's all I can think about.*

My lips pulled into a wide smile that I couldn't resist. Ace's mouth felt incredible against mine, especially with his powerful arm around my waist. It wasn't an appropriate time to say anything back, so I stashed my phone in my pocket.

Evan watched me the whole time. "So, are you dating Ace?"

My head snapped in his direction at the comment,

wondering if he had the nerve to read the message on my phone. "You already asked me that."

"And I never got an answer."

"I told you you didn't deserve one." I didn't want to be hostile when Evan and I were doing well in our new co-parenting relationship, but I wouldn't put up with that kind of disrespect. He didn't get to leave me for someone else then question me about who I was fucking.

"I'm just asking in a friendly way. Curious to know who my girls are spending time with."

"Of course they spend time with Ace, whether I'm dating him or not."

Evan continued to stare at me like he wasn't satisfied with that response. "He used to have a thing for you when we were younger. I wondered if he would make a move after I left."

"Why do you care, Evan?" I thought I detected a hint of jealousy, but that would be ludicrous. This man ended our marriage so he could be with someone else—who happened to be a weirdo.

"Of course I care. Why wouldn't I?"

I didn't want to talk about this anymore. It was strange and uncomfortable. I only saw him as the father of my children, and I no longer possessed any other affection for him. I would always love him, in a way, but I'd made my peace with our divorce. Now I just wanted to be civil partners. Nothing more. "How's work?"

Evan didn't answer, knowing I was just trying to change the subject.

The bell rang, and the girls finally got out of class.

Thank god.

They both ran up to their father like it was the greatest thing in the world seeing him there—even though I picked them up every damn day. They shared hugs and then talked his ear off on the way back to the car.

I drove back to the house without barely getting a hello from my own daughters. They talked about the school day and what they learned in their science classes. Evan seemed genuinely interested in everything they had to say.

We got back to the house, and the girls kept running their mouths.

"Can Daddy stay for dinner?" Rose asked.

"Can you?" Lily asked her father.

Ace wasn't coming over until later, so I didn't see why that would be a problem. And I wanted Evan to spend as much time with the girls as possible. Unlike his girlfriend, I wasn't evil. "Of course your father is welcome."

Evan smiled at my response. "If it's okay, I'd love to stay."

"Great." We went inside, and I got dinner ready while Evan helped them with their homework. For a second, it made me sad because this was exactly what we used to do. Evan helped with their schoolwork while I focused on the laundry and dinner. He helped them get ready for bed while I did the dishes and vacuumed the living room. It was still chaotic, but I didn't feel quite as alone. "Dinner's ready." I set the kitchen table, and we all gathered around to eat.

Evan's phone kept ringing, but he chose to ignore it, hitting a button through his jeans and not even looking at it. When it happened three more times, he finally pulled out his phone and turned it off.

I assumed that meant it was Rebecca—and she wasn't happy he was here.

It was the first time we'd had dinner together at the table since Evan left me, and it made me realize how much I missed it. I missed having the four of us together. I missed being happily married before Rebecca came into his life.

Everything was perfect until that one day he laid eyes on her.

If that hadn't happened, this would be another normal evening.

Before I could get choked up about it, I asked the girls about their homework to change the direction of my thoughts. I refused to let Evan think I missed him. I refused to let him know I was still hurt.

I refused to let him win.

WE'D JUST FINISHED DINNER WHEN SOMEONE KNOCKED ON the door.

That could only be one person.

Evan eyed the door then turned to me, accusation in his eyes.

It would be easy, even satisfying, if I told him I was sleeping with someone else. But I held on to my stubbornness, refusing to stoop to that level. The second I did, it would mean I cared about hurting him, and that didn't paint me in a good light.

I left the dishes in the sink then answered the door.

Ace stood there in jeans and a blue hoodie, looking handsome with his styled hair and sexy grin. "I know I'm early, but I got tired of waiting."

When I looked at him, I forgot about the fact that Evan was still sitting at the kitchen table. I probably should have told Ace to come back later, but he shouldn't have to leave just because my ex was there. That wasn't fair to either of us.

Now Evan would know beyond a doubt Ace and I were something of an item.

"Come in. I have leftovers if you're hungry."

"No, thanks. I had a protein shake for dinner."

"What kind of dinner is that?" I asked with a chuckle. I stepped aside so he could come in.

"The kind that keeps me looking like this." He patted his rock-hard stomach and stepped into the house. It took him a second to realize Evan was sitting at the kitchen table. Ace's eyes landed on him, and he stared him down before he recovered from his subtle surprise.

This should be fun.

But Evan was probably going to head home soon anyway. He had a jealous girlfriend waiting for him. "Can I get you a beer?"

"Sure," Ace answered.

I grabbed a bottle from the fridge and popped off the cap before I handed it to him.

Ace stood there and took a drink, obviously caught off guard that Evan was there.

Evan stared at him without saying anything. The girls were in the living room with their toys, but nobody was watching them at this point.

Geez, it was tense.

Ace walked into the kitchen and finally made the first move. "What's up, man?" He sat down at the opposite end of the table, brushing it off and acting cool.

"Just spending time with the girls. What about you?" Evan couldn't hide the accusation in his expression, knowing exactly why Ace would stop by at eight in the evening just before the girls went to bed.

Ace took a long drink of his beer. "Just stopping by."

Evan kept staring at him.

Ace didn't blink, holding the look without flinching.

I was witnessing a standoff right in the middle of my

kitchen. "Well, I should put the girls to bed. It was nice seeing you today, Evan. The girls really liked the surprise."

Evan reluctantly tore his gaze away from Ace, not wanting to drop his guard. "Let me put the girls to bed."

I hated putting them down. It was one of the biggest hassles of the day. If I let them be, they'd be running around until midnight. "Be my guest."

"Awesome." Evan left the table and walked into the living room. The girls didn't give him any argument at all, doing exactly as they were told and going with him down the hallway.

That was a pet peeve of mine, something all moms probably had to deal with. I was the one who was always there to take care of them, but they gave me attitude because they didn't like being disciplined. Their father was the one who ran off with another woman and was never around, but they worshiped the ground he walked on. Hopefully, they would appreciate me one day.

Ace finally dropped his defensive posture and turned his soft gaze on me. "Evan dropped by again?"

"Yeah. He was waiting for me at the house when I got home from work. We picked up the girls together and had dinner. He's been here all day."

"If I'd known, I wouldn't have stopped by so early."

"Ace, you're welcome to come over whenever you want. I don't care if he's here."

He gave me that sexy expression without even trying. "Yeah? Because I can tell he knows about us."

"Don't care if he does."

His expression lightened, a small smile coming onto his lips. "Good to know."

Evan returned a few minutes later with his hands in the

pockets of his slacks. "Rose needed a story before bed. Lily was out the second her head hit the pillow."

"Sounds about right." I left the table and walked Evan to the door. "They always put up a fight before bedtime, but they fall asleep so easily once they're tucked in."

"Yeah, I remember."

Sometimes I forgot he'd witnessed all of that. He'd been gone for a year, so I was used to it just being the three of us. I brushed off his comment and opened the front door. "I'll see you around."

He took another look at Ace before he stepped out. "How long has this been going on?'

I knew what he was referring to, and I was surprised he had to audacity to question me about it—again. I stepped out and shut the door behind me. "Why do you keep asking me about it, Evan? When you told me you were in love with another woman and wanted a divorce, I didn't ask when it started. I didn't ask when you began to sneak around. So what makes you think you can ask about my personal life?"

Evan rubbed the back of his neck as he looked through the front window. "I'm sorry, you're right. I just...I guess I'm jealous. It's weird for me to see you with someone else."

"It's weird for *you*?" I couldn't keep the exasperation out of my voice. He had a lot of nerve saying that to me. My temper immediately flared, and the rage circulated through my veins before it landed in my heart. "We've been divorced for a year. I waited a lot longer to move on than you did, that's for sure."

His shoulders immediately slumped with the weight of my blow. "I'm not saying it's right. I'm just telling you how I feel. We were married for eight years."

"And you left me for someone else." I said it as calmly as I could, even though my heart was breaking all over again. "I gave you my heart and our children, but that wasn't good enough. You left anyway."

He bowed his head. "I know…"

"So if I want to be with Ace, it's really none of your concern. You need to mind your own business, Evan."

He continued to stare at the ground, his hands in the pockets of his slacks. It didn't seem like he was leaving anytime soon. "I guess things have been different lately. I feel like I just woke up from a dream or something…"

I had no idea what he was talking about. "What's that supposed to mean?"

He raised his head and faced me head on. "I can't explain it… I was going down a path, but now I don't remember how I got there."

Still didn't know what he was saying. "Evan, you should go home. You're tired."

"I'm always tired," he said with a sigh.

I didn't want to keep having this cryptic conversation out in the cold. I had a beautiful man waiting inside for me, a man who would wipe away the thought of Evan the second his hands were on me. Ace wasn't just my lover, but one of my closest friends. Whenever we were together, I felt safe.

Sitting outside and talking to Evan just made me feel lost. "Good night, Evan." I walked back into the house without waiting for him to say it back. I was officially done with this conversation.

I walked into the kitchen and found Ace at the table where I left him.

Ace didn't ask anything, but his eyes were heavy with curiosity.

I changed the subject before the conversation could even start. "How'd it go with Blade?"

"I haven't gone yet. He gets off work at ten."

"Oh."

"Do you think Sara can watch the kids for a few hours?"

I sat down and pulled out my phone. "I haven't had a chance to ask, but she's always interested in extra money." I pulled out my phone and texted her before I left it on the table.

Ace drank his beer in silence, the muscles of his forearms shifting every time he tilted the bottle to his lips. "She won't even need to do anything but sit on the couch and watch TV. They're already asleep."

"Easiest money I've ever heard of."

Ace continued to drink his beer, his eyes on me.

"Why do you keep staring at me?"

"When something is beautiful, you look at it, right?"

A restrained smile crept onto my lips. "You know you're gonna get laid. You don't need to feed me a line."

"It's not a line. I don't use lines. In my experience, they don't work."

Ace didn't need lines because he was the sexiest guy in this town. He could land any woman he wanted without even doing anything. "Did he say anything about me?"

I didn't want to tell Ace the truth, but I wasn't sure why. I guess Evan annoyed me with his questions. He had no right to expect anything from me after what he did. It opened a can of worms, and I didn't want to bring that drama out into the world. "No."

My phone lit up with a message. "Sara said she can do it."

"Awesome. I'm gonna get some liquor in you and see what happens."

"You're gonna get between my legs whether I'm sober or drunk."

He smiled. "Good to know."

8

BLADE

Little Napoli was impossible to get into without a reservation, but since I knew the owner, he managed to squeeze me into a table. I was there first, making sure I was early so I would make a good impression when she walked in. Besides, she'd probably look cute as hell, and I wanted the best seat in the house.

She finally walked inside at seven on the dot and scanned the sea of tables in a long-sleeve royal blue dress with a subtle print of black spots along the fabric. She wore leggings underneath and a pair of shiny black flats. Anytime I saw her clothing, she looked distinctly different from everyone but undeniably classy.

And not to mention, sexy.

I shook it off then stood up, making sure I didn't gawk at her like an idiot this time. I got the woman on a date, so the hard work was done. Now I had to be cool and laid-back, making her laugh and showing her a good time. I'd never been nervous with a woman before, but this chick gave me serious chills.

She spotted me when I stood, probably because I was six three and impossible to miss. She smiled, bright red lipstick on her mouth that contrasted against her fair skin. Her dark hair was in a curtain of soft curls, and she wore the same diamond earrings I'd seen her in before.

When we were close together, my hand moved around her waist, and I gave her a soft kiss on the cheek. A hug might have been more appropriate, but I didn't think twice about it. This was a date, and it wasn't like I kissed her on the mouth right away.

She didn't react to the touch, so I assumed it was okay. If she really was French, the greeting should have been customary to her. She sat across from me, and I followed suit.

Now that I had the date, I wasn't sure what to do while I was on it. There was something about this woman that made my stomach tie up in knots. I wasn't intimidated by her, just fascinated. I was immensely attracted to her, but I also adored her personality—at least what I'd seen of it. "I was going to order a bottle of wine for the table. What do you like? White or red?"

"Both."

"What a coincidence. I do too. How about a Bordeaux?"

"Looks like we have the same taste in wine."

Perfect. I ordered with the waitress then turned my attention back to my date. She was the most beautiful woman in the room, which was saying something because there were a lot of pretty girls around. A few men stared, and if she were my girl, I wouldn't let them stare for long. Showing her signs of my jealousy wasn't a great first impression, so I dismissed it for now.

"I'm glad we got a table," she said. "I rarely come here because I always forget to make reservations."

I almost mentioned I knew the owner, but I thought that would make it seem like I was bragging, so I didn't say anything. "Looks like we got lucky. I'm a big fan of the lasagna. That's probably what I'll get."

"Good choice. I usually get the spaghetti and meatballs. I'm pretty simple."

"Simple but with good taste."

The waitress returned with our bottle and poured the wine. Celeste swirled it before she smelled it and took a drink. "That's good."

I did the same and savored the bold flavor on my tongue. "I like it."

She took another drink before she set her glass on the table.

I didn't want to ask her anything too serious. That made first dates feel like an interrogation. "So, did you make that slab pie yourself?"

She smiled. "The one you bought this morning?"

"Yeah."

"Not personally. But we make it in-house."

"It was amazing. But I wish I hadn't tried it because now I want to eat it every day."

"You only live once, right? Eat pie every day. Who cares?"

She was definitely my kind of woman. "I think Gandhi said something like that."

"Yeah," she said with a laugh. "He was a big pie eater."

I chuckled, feeling a little more relaxed now that the date was going well. "How long have you been working there?"

"I opened the coffee shop three years ago. I usually come around in the summer and fall to keep an eye on things. Besides, France and all of Europe is overrun by tourists then, so it's nice to get away."

She owned the place? "That's awesome. Do you use French recipes for everything?"

"Yep. My nana taught me about baking and her love of coffee. It's been ingrained in my blood. I was here over the summer for college one year, and I decided to open a place of my own. It's been doing well for years now."

"That's really cool. I own a few restaurants too."

"You do?" Her eyes lit up in excitement. "Which ones?"

"Amelia's Place—"

"Oh my god, I love that place. Best pancakes ever."

"Thanks," I said with a smile. "I try not to eat there too often because it makes me fat."

"What other places?"

"Hippopotamus Café."

"I love that place too."

"And Olives. It's a Mediterranean place—"

"I know what you're talking about. That place is awesome too. How do you manage so many places?"

"Well, I work with a group of friends. We own everything together. It can be chaotic, but at the same time, it would be impossible to handle all of that on my own. Plus, it's a lot of fun to do as a group. Makes us spend a lot of time together."

"That's so cool." Her slender fingers were wrapped around the stem of her wineglass, and there was already a lipstick mark from where her mouth had been. "Really impressive. Good for you."

"Thanks."

"Looks like we have a lot in common."

"I guess so. But I'm not French, unfortunately. I grew up in Monterey."

"I love Monterey, especially the aquarium."

"What part of France are you from?"

"Paris," she answered. "One of the most beautiful cities in the world. Carmel reminds me a lot of home, actually. I think that's why I like it so much."

"So you're only here for the season, and then you go back?"

"Yeah."

I hardly knew this woman, and I was already disappointed that she was leaving. There was still a few months of autumn left, but that would pass in the blink of an eye. We hadn't even ordered our food yet, and I was thinking months into the future.

What was wrong with me?

I finally forced myself to say something. "That's cool. Do you have any friends or family here?"

"Just people that I've met here. In France, everything is so busy because tourists come from all over the world. The streets are crowded and restaurants are overrun. It's very hectic. A lot of Europeans travel elsewhere for the holidays because it's so saturated. It's pretty normal."

I didn't let the sadness sink into my gut. All I could have with Celeste was a few months of good sex and nice conversation until she returned the following summer. Normally, I would be ecstatic at the thought of a no-strings-attached relationship, but now I was just bummed out. There was something special about her. I knew it the first time I laid eyes on her. "It gets crowded here in the summer too, but not to that extent."

"Because it's a small town," she said. "Not enough parking for hundreds of thousands of people, thankfully."

I was grateful the waitress returned to take our orders, giving me a second to process what I'd just learned about Celeste. This relationship had a deadline, so it could never really be a relationship, just a fling.

Whatever. I'd take what I could get.

The waitress left, leaving us to our quiet table with a single white candle burning on the surface. Celeste swirled her wine before she took another drink, innately sexy with the slightest movements. Sometimes a strand of hair fell to her cheek, and I wanted to pull it away with my fingers.

"Have you ever traveled to France?" she asked.

"Actually, no. I've never been to Europe at all."

"You should take a trip sometime. If I'm around, I'm happy to give you a tour."

I smiled. "Maybe someday. I'm always so busy with work I rarely travel anywhere, as sad as that is."

"Well, you have the rest of your life. Don't worry about it too much."

It was easy not to have a conversation when I was entertained just looking at her. She had a natural light in her eyes that reminded me of a heavenly glow. It was probably just the candle reflecting in her eyes, but it seemed like a lot more to me.

I found it brave that a beautiful woman could travel to another country alone for months at a time and run a business. The cities along the coast were perfectly safe, but it was still dangerous. I respected her for that and knew I wasn't dealing with the average woman. It was already obvious she was extraordinary. I didn't start my businesses on my own. I needed help because it was very complicated. She must be a natural.

We sat at the table in silence for a few minutes, and I knew I needed to say something and take control of the conversation. I was normally a lot better at this sort of thing, but she was a whole different kind of woman. She had killer looks, killer style, and killer intelligence. "Does your family live in Paris?"

"My father and my stepmother do. My brother is in Italy right now, working on graphic design for a wine company. He's a few years older than I am."

She didn't mention her mother, so I didn't ask.

"My father and I aren't very close. We just happen to live in the same city, and never see each other. But I see my brother all the time. We're really close."

"Has he ever visited you in Carmel before?"

"No, but he's thinking about it. I've been pressuring him to do it for a while. Hopefully, he comes around."

"What do you do you in France? Do you own another business there?"

"Yeah, I have a café in Paris. It's similar to the one here, but much smaller. It's not a big tourist location, so it's mostly locals, which I like. I have a lot of regulars who enjoy their coffee in the morning while they read their newspaper. It's nice getting to know people and having a sense of community even though you have nothing in common except for the love of a beautiful morning."

"That's cool. You have someone oversee it while you're gone?"

"Yeah, I have a manager. All of the regulars disappear when the tourists arrive, so it doesn't feel the same. No matter how many tourists there are here, the locals always stay put, I've noticed."

Her life was fascinating to me. "Anything else back at home?" I wondered if she had a boyfriend, but I doubted she would be on a date with me right now if she did.

"I have a lot of friends in the city. That's usually who I spend time with. Of course, they go visit family in other places on the holidays."

"If everyone leaves France every summer, how do businesses stay open?" I asked with a laugh.

"They don't," she said seriously. "Lots of executive places close down. Or employees work remotely."

"Wow. I can't even imagine what that would be like here." Everyone was always moving at the speed of light here and barely took the time to take a breath.

"Do you have family nearby?"

"My parents are in Monterey. My brother is too."

"That's nice. So they're just down the street."

"Unfortunately," I said with a chuckle. "My mom still calls me almost every day like I live in a different country. When I moved to Carmel, she cried." I rolled my eyes because it was ridiculous. We were less than ten minutes apart.

A distinct sadness came into Celeste's eyes that she couldn't hide. The candle didn't reflect in her gaze anymore. Like a draft had come into the restaurant, it was extinguished.

Did I say the wrong thing? "I'm sorry. Did I offend you?"

"No, of course not." She brushed it off and drank her wine. "My mom and I used to be really close. She used to call me all the time and drive me nuts. But the second she stopped calling me...I missed it."

Now I felt like an ass, not appreciating what I had. "Did she pass away?"

"A few years ago. My dad remarried overnight. It was the summer I came to Carmel and opened my café. I just needed a break from everything, so I got on a plane and took off."

Even though I barely knew her, I was genuinely sad for her. "I'm sorry to hear that."

"It's okay," she said. "It's been a few years now. But when you lose a parent, you never really get over it."

And I had two of them who still loved each other as

much as the day they got married. I felt like an idiot for complaining about my mother's clinginess. I loved her to death, of course. She just suffocated me sometimes, but at least she was there.

I'd have to watch what I said for the rest of the night if I wanted this to end well. I didn't care about hooking up with her when dinner was over. All I wanted was a second date.

And hopefully a third.

WE GOT ICE CREAM ON OCEAN STREET AND WALKED ALONG the white lights as we licked our cones. The mood picked up noticeably once we had food in our bellies, and we didn't mention her family again.

She got French vanilla and I got chocolate, polar opposites. But she looked cute when she ate, swiping her tongue across the cold ice cream before pulling the goodness into her mouth. Since I was a dude, I couldn't stop picturing her tongue moving across the head of my dick in the exact same way.

Don't judge me; I'm a guy. That's the kind of stuff we think about.

We walked along, passing a few couples who were out to dinner together and standing outside restaurants waiting for their tables. It was a warm night, and a breeze was nonexistent. I would have asked if she wanted to walk along the beach, but it was too dark for that.

We passed Olives, seeing the packed restaurant and the workers bustling around.

"Hey, that's your place." She looked through the window as she continued licking her ice cream cone.

"Yep. And I'm glad I'm not inside."

She chuckled. "Looks like it's packed."

"Which is great for me." I finished my cone and tossed the waxed paper into the garbage.

She finished hers a few moments later and threw her napkin into the trash. "That was good. I haven't had ice cream in a long time."

"Because you're eating pie all the time," I teased.

"Guilty," she said with a chuckle.

We reached the next corner and were running out of places to go. I wasn't going to be forward and invite her over to my place. She seemed to be having a good time with me, but I was going to blow it by making a reckless assumption. "I had a great time tonight. Thanks for having dinner with me."

"I had a great time too." She faced me, her clutch tucked under her arm. She was over a foot shorter than me, and that added to her distinct cuteness. I liked short women. Something about their petiteness revved my engine.

My natural instinct was to slide my hand into her hair and kiss her right here on the corner. If people passed on the sidewalk, so be it. I wanted to circle my other arm around her waist and pull her into my chest, feeling the soft skin she was bound to have. I wanted this woman to take my breath away, to leave me hot and bothered so I would think about her for the rest of the night.

But I didn't do that. She hadn't given me a clear sign that she wanted to be kissed, and I didn't want to cross a line if one had been drawn. "I hope we can go out again."

"Me too."

Yes. "I'll see you soon, then." I purposely kept it cool, not wanting to be too forward with her. Women as beautiful as her got more attention than they wanted, and the last thing I wanted to do was suffocate her. I'd stop by her café sometime during the week and ask her out, but I'd definitely wait a little while. She was only in the city for a few more months, but I couldn't rush it. "Good night."

"Good night." She continued to stand in place, like she had more to say.

I leaned in and gave her a hug, feeling the warmth move directly into my cock. I couldn't touch her without getting hard, so I quickly pulled away before she could feel my length through my jeans. The embrace ended a lot sooner than I wanted it to, but it was necessary. I turned away and walked the opposite direction.

"Blade?"

I turned around, hoping she couldn't see my hard-on in the front of my jeans. "What's up?"

She closed the gap between us then circled her arms around my neck. She rose on her tiptoes and kissed me, her luscious body pressed right against mine.

Now I didn't give a damn what she felt.

I gripped her hips and pulled her into me, deepening the kiss and feeling her just the way I imagined. My mouth caressed hers, and I even gave her my tongue, escalating the kiss to R-rated even though we were in public.

She breathed into my mouth, her desire matching mine. Her tits felt perfect against my chest, and I wanted to squeeze them both in my large hands. She relied on my stance to support herself since she was still on the tips of her toes.

I wanted her to feel me, to know how much I wanted her. And I wanted her to know I could rock her world if she let me.

The kiss went on longer than it should, and it was a stroke of luck that no one was nearby. She was the first one to pull away, licking her lips as she moved back. A haze was in her eyes, just like I knew she'd see in mine. "I'm sorry...I just wanted a kiss. Didn't know it would turn into that."

"I did." I pressed my forehead to hers, my hands still on her hips. I felt a surge of attraction the second I laid eyes on her. It was no surprise our chemistry was combustible.

"I should go," she whispered. "Before I do anything else."

I'd take her back to my place right now if she wanted, but I wasn't going to persuade her to make it happen. When she was ready, it would happen. I could be patient. "Probably a good idea." I kissed the corner of her mouth and dropped my hands. "Good night, Celeste."

She reluctantly let me go, the ghost of the kiss still in her eyes. "Good night, Blade."

WHEN I WALKED INTO THE BAR HOURS LATER, I HAD THE biggest and dumbest grin on my face.

Cypress was the first one to spot me at the table. He sat beside Bree, and they both had big glasses of beer in front of them. "Someone got laid."

Amelia turned around in her chair and looked at me. "With a grin like that, I think he got a blow job."

Ace chuckled. "Spill it."

I joined my friends at the table and didn't bother getting a drink. I was drunk off that kiss with Celeste. "Dude, she is awesome. Like, superawesome."

"Superawesome?" Bree repeated. "Are you five, and she's an action figure?"

I ignored her. "She's French. She owns that coffee shop and bakery right next to Hippopotamus Café."

"Oh, I've been there," Amelia said. "They have the best pie."

"I know," I said. "I had a piece."

Ace winked. "Bet you did."

"So she's from France?" Bree asked. "What part?"

"Paris," I said. "And she's got the sexiest accent ever. I love hearing her talk. It's like listening to porn."

Bree rolled her eyes. "That's romantic."

"You really like this girl, huh?" Cypress asked. "Are you gonna see her again?"

"Yeah," I said. "I'm gonna swing by in a few days and ask her to dinner."

"Why don't you just ask her tomorrow?" Amelia asked.

Ace shook his head. "No. Go slow. If you move too fast, she'll think you're obsessed or desperate."

"Or just really into her," Bree said.

Cypress put his hand on her wrist and shook his head. "Leave it to the pros, sweetheart."

It was nice seeing them together again, but I was too obsessed with my own life to care at the moment. "She's really smart, sweet, and funny too. She's, like, the perfect woman."

"And you didn't cross home plate?" Ace asked. "What happened?"

"I didn't want to push it," I answered. "I really want a second date."

"Aww..." Amelia smiled at me. "How sweet."

"That is cute," Bree said.

"I tried to walk away, but she was the one who kissed me good night," I said. "So hot."

"Sounds like she's into you too," Ace noted.

"When do we get to meet her?" Amelia asked excitedly.

The fact that Celeste was only here half the year complicated things. She would never be my girlfriend or a member of our group. "Probably never."

"Why not?" Bree asked. "We've always been nice to your girlfriends."

"And I never hit on them," Ace added.

"Well..." I spotted Lady near the doorway and assumed she was there for Ace. I had taken the last remaining chair, so I should probably pull up another one. But then I saw her walk to the other side of the restaurant and join a few girls. She saw Ace, but she didn't acknowledge him. "Uh, Ace. What's going on with you and Lady?" I nodded to the corner where she was sitting.

Ace glanced then turned back to us. "We stopped seeing each other."

Amelia stiffened, and her eyes popped open in surprise.

"When did that happen?" Cypress asked. "I thought you guys were cool."

Ace shrugged then crossed his arms over his chest. "Wasn't feeling it. She started asking about being serious, so I cut her loose. Not much more to say."

Cypress pressed him. "What about—"

"We're talking about Celeste right now." I hit both of my palms against the table. "All we ever talk about is your love lives. Now it's my turn." I pointed at my chest. "I've got an awesome girl, better than any other chick you guys have brought around."

"Just Ace," Cypress said. "I've never brought anyone around."

Bree didn't look at him, but a hint of a smile was on her lips.

"What else is there?" Amelia asked, no longer stiff.

"Well...she's only here for a few months. Then she goes back home to Paris where she has her other café." It was a deathblow when she told me. Repeating it out loud was even more difficult.

"She's only here through the fall?" Ace repeated. "Like, six months out of the year?"

"That's it?" Cypress asked incredulously.

"Yeah," I said with a sigh. "It really sucks."

"And she does that every year?" Amelia asked.

"Yeah," I answered. "It didn't seem like she had any intention of ever changing her mind. All her family and friends live there."

"So that means this is just a fling, then?" Ace asked. "That's not so bad. And you know she'll always be around next year to hook up."

"I wasn't really looking for a fling when I asked her out," I said honestly. "So now I'm gonna have to make sure I don't start to like her too much. It'll bite me in the ass if I do. I finally found a girl who doesn't bore me, and she's unavailable. Why do I have the worst luck?"

"I'm sorry, Blade." Bree moved her hand over my shoulder, consoling me the only way she knew how. "You'll find the right one eventually, probably when you least expect it."

"Yeah," Amelia added. "Don't be discouraged."

"And this French babe may not be as great as you think," Ace said. "Maybe when you get to know her better, she'll be flawed like everyone else, and you'll lose interest anyway."

"Maybe." But I highly doubted it.

9

Cypress and I walked home in the dark, using our phones as flashlights since there were no streetlights. When we approached his house, Dino's head was visible in the front window as he stood on his hind legs to look out.

Cypress shook his head. "He knows better than that..."

"Leave him alone. He just misses you."

"Misses you too." Cypress stopped in front of his house, his arms by his sides. He glanced at the window before he turned back to me. "Since tomorrow is Sunday...you wanna sleep over, and I'll make breakfast in the morning?"

"Breakfast, huh? Like what?"

A grin stretched across his face. "Pancakes, bacon, and toast."

"Ooh...that sounds pretty good."

"Is that a yes?"

"Like I could say no to bacon."

"Great." He grabbed my hand and walked with me inside the house. The last time I was here, I told him I wanted to call it quits. The smell of his house immediately brought back that memory, and I was surprised to see the table upright again. There was a new vase on top since the last one shattered.

Dino greeted me with a slobbery kiss when I walked inside, and he pawed at my hips.

"Hey, Dino." I kneeled down and scratched him behind the ears. "Who's a good boy?"

He barked.

"You're so cute." I kissed him on the head then followed Cypress into the living room.

"How about I get a fire going, and we watch a movie together?"

"That sounds cozy."

He started the fire and tossed on a few more logs. The TV was above the fireplace, and soon the living room was warm and comfortable. Cypress and I sat together under a warm blanket, and he rested his arm over the back of the couch. Dino lay in his special spot in the corner, happy to have us home.

Cypress flipped through the channels. "How about *Moana*? You love Disney movies, and this came out a few years ago."

"*Moana*?"

"It's about a girl from Hawaii."

"Ooh...that does sound good. But you want to watch a kid's movie?"

"I want to watch anything you want to watch." He turned it on and tossed the remote on the table. "It's not like we're gonna be watching much of it anyway."

Bumps formed all up and down my arms. He'd already asked me to sleep over so I knew what that entailed, but I still got chills when I thought about it. Cypress knew exactly what I liked, and he made love to me in the perfect way. But my throat still went dry, and I felt butterflies in my stomach, as if Cypress and I were a brand-new couple.

The movie played for less than ten minutes before he made a move. He turned his face into mine and kissed me, his strong mouth feeling good against my soft lips. Soon, we were making out in front of the fire, his hand groping my chest through my shirt. His fingers migrated underneath my top and over my bra, gripping my tit with greater control than before. His fingers slid underneath the cotton, and he flicked his thumb over my pebbled nipple.

My hand moved from the back of his neck and down his chest, feeling the concrete under my fingertips. My hand trailed to his jeans, and I got the button undone at the top and his zipper down. Like a teenager, I stuck my hand in his pants and grabbed his hard cock and began to stroke him gently.

His kiss intensified, and he moaned into my mouth while I jerked his nine inches. His hand slid into my unbuttoned jeans, and he found my throbbing clit. He rubbed it hard as he kissed me, getting me off with just his hand.

I jerked him harder and shuddered against his mouth, feeling my body tighten in preparation for a climax. Knowing we were doing something so juvenile as married adults somehow made it sexier.

Cypress must have known I was about to come because he pulled his hand away.

I moaned in protest. "Cypress..."

He yanked his boxers and jeans down to his knees and then helped me get out of my clothes. His long cock lay against his stomach, rock-hard and throbbing to be inside me. When my bottoms were off, he positioned me to straddle his hips and sink onto his length.

I took every inch of him, moaning loudly as he stretched

me like every man should stretch his woman. I took him balls deep and sat still, treasuring the feeling of all nine inches of him.

Cypress moaned louder than I did, and he dug his fingertips into my ass, squeezing my cheeks aggressively. My shoes were still on because I hadn't taken them off, and they sat on either side of his knees, rubbing against his skin every time I made a move.

Cypress's eyes were lidded and heavy as his hands glided up to my chest, and he squeezed my tits through my bra. He ground his hips slightly, his cock rubbing against the sides of my tight channel. "Fuck..."

I hadn't even begun to move yet, and we were both already crippled by how great it felt.

Cypress sat back against the couch and then lifted me up, pulling his length out until only his head was inside. Then he pulled me down again, sliding through my wetness until he was balls deep again. Every time he was completely sheathed, he moaned. "So fucking good..."

When I saw the desire in his eyes, he made me feel sexy. It pushed me to be more adventurous, to be more confident. My hands pressed against his chest, and I used his physique for balance as I moved up and down and rocked my hips at the same time. I took his length over and over, my pussy soaking his cock in my arousal.

Cypress grabbed my hips and controlled their tilt, making me grind my clit against his body at the perfect angle. My nub was on fire, and I panted through the pleasure, forgetting to move when it felt too good.

He pressed his face to mine and kissed the corner of my mouth, his tongue swiping over my bottom lip when he finished. "I love you, sweetheart." He pulled me tighter against him as he thrust up with his hips, taking over the momentum.

When he said those words to me, I didn't know if he expected me to say them back, or if he just wanted to say them. He had a special place in my heart, but I couldn't say I was there just yet. When the moment didn't change, I assumed he was okay with that. All he wanted was for me to know how he felt. Or maybe he fantasized this was another time, back before I hit my head and lost all my memories.

But watching him adore me and listening to him worship me heightened my experience and sent me over the edge. I came with my nails digging into his skin and a moan screaming from my throat. My arousal splashed all over him, soaking him all the way down to his balls. "Cypress..."

"I love watching you come for me." He dug his hand into my hair and gripped me harshly, putting me in the perfect position for him to move harder. He thrust his hips and hit me deeply, giving me all of his length over and over.

I knew he was about to come inside me, so I reached behind me and massaged his sac with my fingertips, giving him the extra touch he needed to explode deep inside me. "I want your come."

"Jesus fucking Christ." He pulled me entirely down his length as he released, filling me with his mounds of seed. He collapsed back against the couch as the blood flushed into his cheeks. His eyes were just as lidded as before, but now his jaw was squared and he looked even more handsome than usual.

I rested against his chest and pressed my face next to his. I was hot and covered in sweat, but I wanted to be near him anyway. I wanted to share this connection that we had, to let it grow into something more. "I liked the movie..."

A ghost of a smile stretched his lips. "Yeah, me too." He

turned off the TV with the remote before he rose to his feet, keeping me attached to him with a single arm. He carried me into his bedroom down the hall, his cock still buried inside me where it belonged.

He laid me down on the bed then pulled off my Keds and socks. He still hadn't pulled out of me yet, and now I wasn't sure if he was going to. Last time I was here, he pumped me with so much come I could barely walk.

He watched my expression as he slowly pulled out of me, his cock still big even when it was soft. He balanced back on his ankles and removed his shirt before he yanked the rest of my clothes off. Once we were naked together, he tugged the sheets over us and got comfortable beside me in bed.

We became tangled up together, one person underneath the sheets with our dog at the end of the bed. The picture frame was still on the nightstand, and his wedding ring sat on his left hand. He'd put it back on once I asked for another chance, and I never imagined how relieved I would feel once he was wearing it again.

"Just so you know, I snore."

I chuckled. "Yeah, I remember."

"Well, it's gotten worse over the years. And Dino snores too."

"Now I wish I snored."

"I don't," he said with a chuckle. He kissed my shoulder then pressed his face into my hair, inhaling my scent. "I miss this so much. It used to be my favorite time of the day."

"Why?"

"We'd make love and talk before going to sleep every night. Just the two of us. No work. No friends. Just us."

My hand moved over his defined knuckles, feeling the hills and valleys of his hands. "It is nice..."

"There are times when I want to bring up something from the past, and I remember you don't have any memory of it. It's hard for me to keep track of things."

"Then maybe you should start from the beginning. I don't mind hearing about how we used to be. What were you thinking of saying?"

He spooned me from behind and kept his face buried in the hair at the back of my neck. Every time he exhaled, some of his breath moved through my strands and grazed against my bare skin. It was warm and sexy, and I found myself looking forward to every breath he took.

"I was going to say there was a time when marriage wasn't important to me. In fact, I didn't want to get married at all. Didn't seem like something I'd be interested in. Even when we were dating the first time, it didn't really cross my mind. And now...I love being married. I love being with you every day and every night. It makes me realize how little I had before since I have so much now. That's something I would think about almost every night while we lay next to each other, that I'm lucky to have this. And now that you're back...I'm happy again."

I was glad I couldn't see his face because I thought I would start crying if I looked at him. It was heartfelt and sweet, and it made me wish I remembered everything we'd been through. It made me wish I could tell him I loved him when he said it first. "I wish I could remember everything."

"It's not your fault," he whispered. "Don't feel bad about it. I'll remember enough for you." He tightened his arm around my waist and pulled me closer into his hard chest. When we were skin to skin like this, I could feel the warmth of his body and the pounding of his heart.

"I'm sorry I've been so difficult, Cypress."

"It's okay," he said quickly. "You've been through a lot. If I lost my memory, I know I would be freaking out."

"You've been very sweet to me, and I've never really given you a chance."

"You're giving me a chance now, and that's all that matters. It's okay if you don't love me right now. It's okay if you don't trust me. Those things will happen in time. I know they will." He pressed a kiss to the back of my neck and snuggled directly behind me.

"Did we talk about having children?"

"Yeah. We wanted to have two kids. One boy and one girl."

"When did we want to have them?"

"Actually, we were about to start trying before your accident. You said you wanted our kids to be close in age to Rose and Lily."

"Oh..." If I hadn't lost my memory, I'd be a mom right now. I could potentially have two kids, or at least one.

"But there's still time. When you're ready, we can have them."

"And we were going to raise them in my house?"

"Yeah. I lived with Amelia until this place went on the market. I went to the owner and told him about the situation, so he let me buy it privately."

"Oh..."

He fell quiet, his breathing growing even behind him.

"Cypress?"

"Hmm?"

"Why did you fight so hard for me? Why didn't you just let me go?" I knew he said he loved me, but I thought there had to be a stronger reason than that. "Eighteen months is a long time. At the time, you thought there was no chance of me recovering. Anyone else would have left."

"Because I love you."

"There has to be more of a reason than that." He spent every day having the same conversation with me. He couldn't move on and date anyone, not when he had a crazy ex living next door.

"You changed my life in the greatest way possible. You gave me happiness, something I never felt before. I owed everything to you. I wasn't going to give up, and I knew you would never give up on me. When you find the one person you're supposed to spend your life with, you realize there's no one else in the world that could ever replace them. It's them, or it's no one."

It was something else I didn't expect Cypress to ever say. He was never this romantic or raw in my memory. But something obviously changed him along the path of our relationship. "So, you believe we're supposed to be together?"

He didn't hesitate before he answered. "Without a doubt."

I turned over and faced him, hooking my leg over his waist and bringing us closer together. That's when I felt his hard cock press against me, his body telling me he already wanted another round.

Cypress looked at me with his pretty blue eyes, his jaw rigid with masculinity. His hand glided up my body, his coarse skin grazing across my softness. There was a connection in the air, and he was just as aware of it as I was.

I turned him to his back as I crawled on top of him. My hands pressed against his chest, and my hair fell over one shoulder as I swung my leg over his hip and sat on his lap. My pussy was right against his length, feeling the hardness that was similar to steel.

Cypress immediately squeezed my hips and watched me grind against his length.

I was ready to take him again, to feel his impressive size inside me. It was the first time I didn't want him just to get off. I wanted to feel him inside me, to stretch me apart as we explored each other in mutual pleasure.

I wanted to make love.

Cypress guided me onto his length with a suppressed moan. Like we hadn't just had sex thirty minutes ago, he was excited all over again. His cock slid through my slickness and fit into my pussy perfectly, stretching me until it was a little painful.

He rolled me onto my back and remained inside me until he positioned himself on top of me. I knew he liked it when I was on top, bouncing hard on his dick, but he obviously wanted to be in control for this round. His hand slid into my hair where it was usually positioned, and he got a fistful of hair before he started to move. "Damn…"

10

I didn't see Ace much that day because we worked in different locations. I hadn't had a chance to ask him about his situation with Lady, but even if I did, I wasn't sure if I had the courage to bring it up at all.

Did it mean anything?

He didn't seem that interested in her to begin with, so probably not. But I still couldn't bring it up. He might think I was jumping to conclusions, that he dumped her so he could be with me exclusively.

That would be a dream.

I walked home from work and spotted Evan outside my house—again.

What the hell was he doing here?

"Evan?" I watched him stand up from the stone steps when he noticed me and slipped his phone into his pocket.

"Hey, Amelia." He walked down the sidewalk and approached me in the front yard, where the two cypress trees stood tall. My car was in the driveway because I never used it for anything. His BMW was at the curb. He looked handsome in his black slacks and collared shirt. No matter how much I despised him, I couldn't forget why I fell for him in the first place. And it was no surprise he could get a woman ten years younger than him—and it wasn't just because he was successful.

"What are you doing here?"

He crossed his arms over his chest and tilted his head. "I thought you said I'm always welcome here."

"I did say that. But you're always here now. Not used to it."

"Well, I was gonna ask if I could pick up the girls from school and take them to the beach."

"You could have called." We didn't need to have all of these face-to-face interactions. I wanted to be partners in parenting, nothing more than that.

"I knew you were at work."

He was smooth. "Well, have fun with the girls. I'm gonna take a shower and open a bottle of wine." I walked around him and headed to the door, looking forward to some alone time. I'd probably hit up Ace and see if he was down for a hookup.

"Why don't you come with us?" He turned around and watched me go.

"I spend every hour with the kids as it is. I want a break." I'd love to do my hair and makeup for once, look particularly sexy and put on some lingerie before I invited Ace over. That was a fantasy I hadn't lived out in a long time.

"Then how about we have dinner together?"

He was spending a lot of time with the kids all of a sudden. "You have time to do all of that? Don't you need to be getting home?"

Evan slid his hands into his pockets and shrugged. "Not really."

I didn't know what that meant, but I didn't want to know. "You can have the kids. Momma is gonna relax." I walked in the house without turning back, immediately jumping in the shower and cranking up the radio.

———

HAIR AND MAKEUP READY, I TEXTED ACE. *WHAT ARE YOU doing? I'm home alone.*

The three dots popped up immediately. *You have my attention.*

And I'm in black lingerie.

The dots barely had a chance to pop up before the words appeared. *Now you have my dick's attention too.*

I took a picture of myself in the mirror, positioning my body to hide all the parts of my figure I didn't like. I sent it to him without adding a caption.

Damn. I'm on my way.

I smiled and read the words a few times, feeling like I was flying on cloud nine. I'd never had the confidence to take a picture of myself and send it to any other guy. Ace was the only one who made me feel good about myself. I didn't just feel like a woman with two kids. I felt like a fantasy.

He was at my house in five minutes, pulling up in his car because walking obviously wasn't fast enough. He came in through the front door and looked me up and down, his eyes greedy. "Even better in person." He backed me up into the door and secured his hands against the wood on either side of me, closing me in. "Kids aren't here?"

"Evan has them for an hour or so."

At the mention of Evan, the heat in his eyes dampened slightly. But the fire picked up again within seconds. "Then let's do this." He scooped me up and held me against the door, his powerful body strong enough to support me without exertion. His lips moved to the hollow in my throat, and he ran his tongue across the skin. "I'm gonna fuck you so hard, baby."

My hands dug into his hair as I closed my eyes. "Please do."

AFTER WE LAY ON THE BED FOR A FEW MINUTES, ACE GOT UP and pulled on his jeans and t-shirt.

I hated to see him leave, but I knew Evan would be home with the girls soon. It was a lot easier to sidestep the conversation by having Ace leave than having him stick around. Of course, if Ace wanted to stay, I wouldn't ask him to go.

Ace watched me as he shoved his phone into his front pocket. "You look hot in lingerie."

"I think that's what it's for—to help women like me look sexy."

He leaned over me on the bed and pressed a kiss to my lips. "You'd look sexy in a brown paper bag." He gave me another kiss before he stood upright. "I should get going. I haven't done laundry in nearly two weeks."

"How do you still have underwear?"

"Turned them inside out."

I chuckled and got dressed. "You need a maid."

"Don't we all?" he asked. "You could be my maid if you dressed like that all the time."

"I don't think I would get anything done with you staring at me."

"True. But in that case, I wouldn't want anything to get

done." He gave my waist a squeeze before he walked into the hallway.

I fixed my hair and my makeup before I walked him to the door. "Thanks for stopping by."

"Anytime." He turned around when he reached the front door. "You know I'm always down to fuck such a beautiful woman."

Another compliment that went straight to my core. "Thanks."

He cupped my cheek and gave me a slow kiss before he pulled away. It was soft and delicate, a direct contrast to the intense way we fucked against the wall in my bedroom. It was nice, making me feel sensual and adored.

He turned to the door. "Bye."

"Why did you stop seeing Lady?" I wanted to cover my face in humiliation for blurting that out. When he teased me with that kiss of his, I did the dumbest things. My heart took over, letting my brain bite the dust.

He halted in place, his hand still on the doorknob. He was quiet, so it didn't seem like he was going to answer.

"Sorry...I was just curious. You know, as a friend."

"There's not much to tell. She wanted something serious, and I didn't."

That was all I was going to get out of him, and I knew it. I was an idiot for thinking there was even a remote possibility that he'd stopped seeing her because of me. When we had great sex, I just assumed it meant as much to him as it did to me. "Oh...I'm here to talk if you need a friend." Actually, I didn't want to hear anything about the women he was screwing.

"Thanks." He finally walked out and got into his car. When he was gone, I shut the door and stood in the entryway, feeling mortified by the stupid thing I'd just done.

How could I be that stupid?

I hoped I hadn't screwed things up with him.

Such a dumb thing to ask.

Ace left just in time because Evan came home with the girls not even two minutes later. He walked them into the house, and the girls both gave me a hug before they went into their bedrooms to drop off their backpacks.

"Did you guys have fun?" I asked. I know I did.

"Yeah," Evan answered. "We went to the beach then got dinner. What did you do?"

"Just hung out...does that mean they don't need dinner?"

"No, they're good." He helped himself to a seat at the kitchen table, obviously having no intention of going anywhere.

I hoped that didn't mean he was sticking around. I purposely didn't offer him anything to drink as a hint. "Were they surprised to see you?"

"They both screamed," he said with a chuckle. He leaned back in the chair and placed one ankle on the opposite knee.

He definitely wasn't going anywhere. I walked to the table and joined him, sitting across from him. "You must be tired."

"No, I feel fine."

Ugh. Was he always this dense, or was he purposely ignoring my hints? "You want a beer?"

"Yeah, that'd be great."

I grabbed one, removed the cap, and placed it on the table in front of him. The sun was beginning to set in the distance, and the light was slowly fading. In another hour, the girls would be in bed, prepared to go to sleep.

I knew Rebecca hated me, so she must not approve of

Evan being here—unless he lied and said he was working late.

The conversation dried up, so there was really nothing to say. But yet, he lingered anyway. Ace and I didn't always talk to each other, but we were great friends so the silence was comfortable. I felt that way about all of my friends. But I didn't consider Evan to be a friend at all. I loved him and always would, but his betrayal removed him from the friend zone permanently.

I wondered why he was sticking around. Maybe he wanted to say goodbye to the girls? Tuck them in like last time? I didn't have a clue. That must be it.

"I left Rebecca."

My head moved in his direction, but I stared at him blankly because I couldn't believe what he'd said. "You left Rebecca?" The best thing I could do was repeat the exact words he said to me.

"Yeah." He stared at his beer while his fingers rested around the bottle.

After he broke up our marriage and betrayed my trust, I'd assumed he would marry her and spend the rest of his life with her. But they didn't even last a year. It was pathetic, and it also made me even angrier. It was worth throwing me away for a relationship that only lasted a year? He obviously didn't know that at the time, but it was still insulting. "Why?" Maybe she cheated or something. Karma had a way of working out like that.

He stared at his beer for another thirty seconds before he sighed and looked up at me. "It was a lot of things. She was overly jealous. She didn't like it anytime I had a client that was female and under forty. She didn't want me to be around my own kids because she didn't want me anywhere near you..."

I guess my hunch was dead-on.

"And then when she texted you...that was the last straw for me. I get that she's jealous, but she had no right speaking to the mother of my kids like that. I knew it was only going to get worse from that point onward."

I hated him for leaving me, but I respected him for standing up for me.

"And...being with her just made me realize what I lost."

My heart stopped.

"I was happy in the beginning, but after a few months, I kept thinking about you. I kept wishing I were watching TV with you on a Sunday afternoon while the girls played with their toys. I wished I were dropping off the girls at school in the morning. I missed getting lunch at Amelia's Place just to see you. The high I had wore off, and reality set in. I thought I could shake it off, but she just clung to me tighter. That's when she became more jealous...when she realized I was unhappy."

I sat there in disbelief, unable to believe Evan had just confessed all those things to me. He made a mistake, and he knew it. Instead of feeling satisfied that karma was on my side, I didn't feel anything at all. It took me a long time to get over Evan, and thinking about how happy he was with someone else was what pushed me forward. If he expected me to say something, he was going to be disappointed.

What the hell should I say to that?

Evan looked at me, watching me with a guarded expression. When I didn't say anything, he spoke again. "I have an apartment in Monterey now."

I was still in shock, but I did a good job hiding that expression from my face. I kept up a stoic appearance, keeping my cards close to my chest.

Evan eventually grew impatient with my silence. "What are you thinking?"

"I don't know what I'm thinking..."

He lowered his eyes in disappointment. "I know it's a far stretch, and I shouldn't even—"

"Then don't," I said calmly. "Don't even go there."

Evan pushed his beer to the side even though it wasn't in the way in the first place. "I made the worst mistake of my life, and I know it. I knew it months ago."

I refused to look at him.

"I miss you."

I'd cried myself to sleep more times than I could count. I'd relied on Cypress to help me with the girls because I was too heartbroken to take care of them. Every day at work, I was just a ghost. The divorce was the most difficult thing I ever had to go through. I lost the man I loved to a woman he had nothing in common with.

"I want to be a family again. I want to come home to you and the girls every night. I want to—"

"Never. Going. To. Happen." I finally focused my eyes on him, keeping my posture rigid and my expression strong.

He stilled at my words, holding my gaze without blinking.

"You made your decision, Evan. You didn't want to work on the marriage. You didn't want to go to counseling. You came home and told me you were in love with another woman. There was no room for discussion. You packed your things and left. That was the end. You have a lot of balls coming into my house and sweeping all of that under the rug."

"I never swept it under the rug. I know I did a terrible thing—"

"And we've moved past it. But we're never, ever getting

back together. I don't care if it's better for the girls. It's not better for me."

He rested his face in his palms and dragged his hands down his face. "You still love me." He raised himself upright again and looked at me.

"I'll always love you, Evan. How can I not love the man who gave me two of the most precious things in my life? But I don't love you the way I did before. I'm not in love with you, and I certainly could never trust you again."

"Well, I love you."

"It's debatable whether you loved me to begin with, Evan."

"Of course I did. I just..."

What kind of explanation could he possibly give me?

"I just got lost."

"You saw a hot woman and left your wife. You traded in the woman with stretch marks from childbirth for a size zero model. That's what happened, Evan. End of story."

He finally fell silent, his argument expired.

"I want to be friends and partners. I want us to be happy for each other. But that's the extent of it."

He rubbed his chin as he thought of his next move. "Is it because of Ace?"

"Is what because of Ace?"

"That you don't want to work this out?"

I raised an eyebrow so far it almost hopped off my face. "You really think the only thing stopping me from getting back together with you is Ace? Uh, no. You really see me as that pathetic? No. The reason why I'm not getting back together with you is because I don't want to. That's all."

"That's not what I meant," he said calmly.

"It sure sounded like it."

"Well, you've never confirmed if you're seeing him or not."

"Because it's irrelevant."

Evan held his gaze on me, hardly blinking. "Whether you're seeing him or not, I'd like for us to be together. I'd like it if we were a family again. I'm sure a guy like him wouldn't want to stand in the way of that."

"A guy like him would love to beat the shit out of you, Evan. That's what all my friends want."

"It didn't seem like it when he came by the office."

My heart moved up my throat then plummeted back down to my stomach. "What?"

Evan looked away. "He came in with the rest of your friends and told me to get my shit together. They told me to step up and be a good father. I wanted to do that anyway, but they gave me the push I needed."

Ace did that without telling me? He went behind my back? "When did this happen?"

"A few weeks ago. So I know he cares about us being a family."

I sat back in my chair and took a breath, trying to wrap my mind around all of this. I couldn't believe Ace interfered in my relationship with Evan without telling me. How could he do that? This whole time I thought I was the one getting through to Evan, but that turned out to be a lie.

"I don't mind taking it slow. I know I really hurt you, and it'll take some time—"

I jumped out of my chair. "Get out of my house, Evan."

He watched me with a hardened stare and didn't move.

"Let me make this clear. I will never, under any circumstance, ever be with you again. What you did was unforgivable, and I deserve better."

"But everyone forgave Cypress for what he did to Bree."

I couldn't believe he'd thrown that in my face. "Not the same thing."

"It's the exact same thing."

"Cypress would never leave his wife and kids the way you did." I marched to the front door. "Get out of my house."

He stayed at the table for a moment before he sighed and stood up. He took his time getting to the entryway, like procrastinating long enough would make me change my mind about us. He finally crossed the door and turned around, wearing a look of apology.

"Just so you know, Ace likes my stretch marks." I slammed the door in his face, probably getting the girls' attention, but I didn't care. I'd never had the chance to slam the door on him before, and now I finally did.

ACE WALKED IN THE DOOR TEN MINUTES AFTER I ASKED HIM to come over. The girls were asleep, so we had our privacy, but I wanted to talk outside just in case the girls heard us yelling at each other.

I pulled him outside and shut the door.

"Baby, what is it? Everything okay?"

For a second, I forgot how angry I was when he called me that. "You went to Evan's work and told him to start coming around again?"

The second the concern washed off his face, I knew his answer.

"And you didn't tell me?"

He tightened his jaw and sighed. "No, I didn't. It wasn't just me. We were all there."

"But I'm sleeping with you, not the others."

"Bree is your sister."

"But I expected this from her. Not you."

"I was just trying to help. And frankly, it worked. There's no reason to be upset."

"I just can't believe you went behind my back and made me think I was the one who got him to change." I was embarrassed that I actually thought my words had any effect on the situation.

"I get that you're mad, but I was just trying to help. If you took two seconds to think about it, you would thank me for it."

I was still mad at him, but I knew I had no right to be. "I'm sorry...he just dropped a bomb on me."

"Why did he tell you that anyway?"

I wasn't planning on telling anyone what Evan said to me. For some reason, I found it embarrassing. Evan already left his girlfriend after a year of being together. That somehow made me look worse. But I was too upset to think straight, and I didn't like to lie to Ace. He was the one person I could be transparent with. "He said he left his girlfriend and wanted to get back together. He made the worst mistake of his life..."

Ace's face transformed into a look I'd never seen before. He didn't look angry or indifferent. It seemed like he'd been punched in the gut. "And what did you say?"

"I told him to get the hell out of my house. If he thinks I'm gonna take him back after what he did, he's an idiot."

Ace stared me down.

I didn't understand his look or his sudden change in mood. Now he was just looking at me. "What?"

"I just...it's a lot to take in."

"I couldn't believe it either. If he's gonna leave me for someone, he better stay with her. They barely lasted a year. Totally pathetic."

"Did he say anything else?"

"Not really. Just that he was sorry, and it was a mistake... blah blah. He says he has an apartment in Monterey now."

Ace crossed his arms over his chest. "Do you still have feelings for him?"

"What kind of question is that?"

"Just a question," he said. "It's only been a year since you got divorced. It hasn't really been that long."

"What are you implying?"

He stepped back and slid his hands into his pockets. "I'm not implying anything. I'm just talking to you as a friend right now. A pretty big life event just happened to you. Your ex-husband, the love of your life, just came back and asked for another chance. It's a pretty big deal."

Sometimes I forgot we weren't together because it was so easy to imagine. When we were in bed, I fantasized that we were more than just good friends. But we were fuck buddies, as he'd made perfectly clear. "He betrayed my trust. He can never get that back."

"Cypress got it back."

"Not the same thing and you know it. Do you want me to get back together with him?" I couldn't stop the pain from escaping in my voice. Did he care so little for me that it really didn't matter to him?

"I didn't say that."

"It sounds like you're implying it."

"He's the father of your children..."

"So what? That obviously didn't mean anything to him. I thought my getting back together with him would piss you off. You should hate him."

"I do hate him, and it would piss me off—but I would understand. You're a family, Amelia. You've got two little girls. I know you're mad at him for what he did, and you have every right to feel that way, but I know you love the guy."

"I *loved* him. Past tense."

"And you always will. I just think you're angry right now, but when that rage passes, you'll feel differently."

"Not a chance."

Ace stepped back again. "I'm sorry for going behind your back. I meant well."

I felt him slipping away from me, putting up a wall between us and shutting me out. "I know, Ace. I'm sorry I got so upset. I just feel stupid. That's all."

"No need to feel stupid. You have a lot of people who love you. You should feel happy."

"I know..."

He rested his hands in his pockets then looked at the ground. "I should go."

I wanted him to stay. I wanted him to stay every single night. I wanted my girls to see him in the morning. I wanted more than this distant relationship. We had so much potential to be something incredible, but his heart wasn't in the right place. If only he loved me, we could have everything I wanted. "Okay." I could tell him how I felt all over again, but it wouldn't change anything. He left Lady, but that was obviously just a coincidence.

"Good night." He didn't kiss me goodbye. He didn't even hug me. He walked to his car and drove away without waiting for me to walk inside.

Something told me things were different between us. When we said goodbye, we were saying bye to more than just the evening. He didn't show his charismatic smile or the affection in his eyes. All of that disappeared instantly.

But why?

11

BREE

The doorbell rang.

My eyes snapped open, and Dino jumped off the bed and darted downstairs, barking in excitement that someone had come to the door.

Cypress rolled over and got comfortable again, keeping his eyes closed.

"Such a protector..." I gave him a gentle kick in the leg.

"You've got Dino, don't you?"

That dog couldn't protect me from a puppy. I pulled on Cypress's boxers and one of my sweaters before I walked downstairs, not sure who I was going to encounter this early in the morning. I needed to get to work, but it was hard to get up when I had a sexy man in bed with me.

I wiped the sleep from my eyes then opened the door. "Amelia? What are you doing here?"

"I need to talk to you." Once she saw Dino, she gave him a pat on the head and walked inside. "I'm assuming you have company..." Her smile held all her accusation.

"Yeah..."

"Good to know." She helped herself to the couch and sat down. "I wouldn't be bothering you if this weren't important."

"What's up?"

Dino hopped on the couch and rested his chin on her thighs. He looked up at her and released a small whine, asking her to pet him.

Amelia immediately obeyed and stroked her hand over his head and down his back.

Dino closed his eyes.

"What happened?" I asked.

She looked down at Dino before she met my gaze. "Evan has been coming by a lot lately…"

"That's great. I'm glad that piece of shit remembers he's a father."

She pressed her lips tightly together, and that told me this conversation went deeper than that. "I thought it was strange that he wouldn't give us the time of day and then he was over all the time. It got to the point where we were seeing him too often. So he told me he left Rebecca, moved to Monterey, and wants to get back together."

My jaw dropped, and a hiss escaped my throat. "You're kidding."

"I wish I were."

"No way!"

She nodded.

I jumped to my feet because I was too pissed to sit down. "He had the balls to actually ask you that?"

"I know, right?" she asked with a chuckle. "I told him it was never going to happen then kicked him out."

My hands moved to my hips, and I started to pace, unable to swallow the rage that burned inside me. "I can't believe that. How long was he with that whore? Like, nine months?"

"About eleven."

I rolled my eyes. "What else did he say?"

"That he made a mistake and misses me. Misses being a family."

"You know what?" I stopped and stomped my foot. "I hate him even more now."

She chuckled. "I know what you mean."

I crossed my arms and kept pacing. "What did he expect? You to be happy and jump back in his arms?"

"Something like that."

"Idiot." I shook my head in disgust before I looked out the window.

"I still haven't processed everything. When he left me for her, I assumed they would spend the rest of their lives together. When we were together, we were happy. We were happy every single day until he met her."

"It was all physical infatuation—and that's not love."

"I think he realized that."

"Well, he learned the hard way." I looked at my sister, realizing ranting wasn't helping the situation. This was about her, not me. "How do you feel about all of this?"

"I don't know," she whispered. "I'd be lying if I said I hadn't dreamt about this happening a few times, just to get some vengeance. But now that it did happen, I haven't gotten any satisfaction out of it. I'm hurt, actually. He ended our marriage for a yearlong fling. It makes me feel like our marriage wasn't that important in the first place."

Her thoughts made complete sense to me. "I know what you mean."

"I know I'll always love Evan because he's been in my life for so long. I was married to that man for eight years. I still find his socks and boxers around the house, stuffed in drawers or behind the dryer. I still make sure the cap to the toothpaste is on because of how much it used to annoy him when I left it open. It's difficult to erase eight years of memories in such a short amount of time. And I do miss being a family. I miss the routine Evan and I had. Plus, having him around made raising kids so much easier."

I studied her gaze as she laid out all of her feelings. Vulnerable and honest, she was opening up to me. I understood the situation with Evan wasn't black and white, just like how my relationship with Cypress was complicated. There was no perfect way to approach the problem.

"But I don't think I could ever trust him again. I don't think I could ever forgive him."

I hoped not. She had Ace desperate for her affection, and she didn't even realize it. If she turned down Evan for good, maybe Ace would be honest about his feelings. My jaw tightened anxiously because I wanted to tell her everything Ace told me, but my vow kept my tongue in my mouth. "I wouldn't blame you."

"I don't see why we can't be a family even if we remain divorced. People do it all the time."

"Exactly. So that means you aren't gonna give Evan another chance?"

She shook her head. "No. He doesn't deserve it."

Phew. What a relief.

Cypress woke up and made his way down the stairs in just his sweatpants. His hair was messy, and he moved like a zombie, still half asleep. With eyes lidded and heavy, he wiped the sleep from the corners then walked up to me. "Morning, sweetheart." His arm circled my waist, and he kissed me on the cheek.

"Morning," I whispered back.

He walked into the kitchen and poured himself a cup of coffee. "Morning, Amelia."

She grinned and kept her eyes on me. "Morning, Cypress."

He walked outside and shut the door behind him. Patio furniture was arranged in the backyard, and he sat down in one of the lounge chairs and enjoyed his coffee under the blue sky. The sun was creeping over the fence and rising higher as the morning progressed.

I stared at Amelia's grin and knew exactly what she was thinking.

"Looks like you slept well last night."

"Not quite. Cypress and Dino snore."

She rolled her eyes. "You probably weren't sleeping anyway."

No, not really. I brushed off her comment silently, my cheeks reddening.

"I'm glad you guys are working it out. There's been a lot of bumps, but I really think Cypress is worth the heartache."

My feelings were complicated, but I definitely felt the love growing in my heart. I missed him when we weren't together, and I loved the way my sheets smelled now that he'd slept over. Having a big man share my bed was one of the greatest comforts I'd ever known. He was so warm and hard. I loved it. "Yeah...we're trying."

She pulled back her sleeve and eyed her watch on her wrist. "I should get going. Sara has a hair appointment, so she can't stick around too long."

"Okay. Call me if you want to talk more about it."

"You know I will." She stood up and kissed me on the cheek before she walked out. "But I'll try not to bug you for the next few hours. You know, because you have company." She winked then shut the door behind her.

When my sister was gone, I walked out onto the back patio and found Cypress sipping his coffee while he stared at his phone. Dino trailed behind me then found a good place to pee behind one of the bushes.

Cypress set down his mug and looked at me, looking more handsome than he had any right to at that hour. "Everything okay with Amelia?"

"Yeah." I drank from his mug then sat on his lap and hooked my arm around his shoulders.

He looked up at me and smiled as his hand grazed my thigh. "Now I'm comfortable."

I sipped his coffee again and felt his erection underneath my legs. "She told me Evan wants her back."

His hand stilled on my thigh, and his smile faded away. "He said that?"

"Yeah." I took another drink then set the mug down.

"That douchebag has a lot of nerve. She said no, right?"

"Yeah."

"Thank fucking god," he said with a sigh. "That piece of shit doesn't deserve another chance." His face immediately tinted red, and he became hostile, the vein in his forehead bulging. The veins in his forearms constricted as both of his hands formed fists. "If they didn't have kids, I'd have no problem killing him."

"I'm not a fan of him either."

"So what happened to that woman he was seeing?"

"He broke up with her. Now he's staying in Monterey."

He shook his head, his jaw tense. "What was the problem with her? Too immature? Did she leave him?"

"He said she was too jealous, and he missed Amelia. So he broke it off with her, and now he wants to be a family again."

"Never gonna happen," he snapped. "You don't get to be

a family again after you abandon them once. That's not how it works." He was even more worked up about it than I was.

"Amelia is smart. She won't go back to him."

"She better not. I'd have to give her a piece of my mind if she did."

I gave him a hard look, conveying my thoughts because I didn't have the ability to say them out loud.

Cypress picked up on the accusation. "It's not the same thing. Abandoning your wife and children is much different than having a slipup with an ex one time. I'm not saying my actions were acceptable, but they aren't comparable."

I let it go before it launched us into another uncomfortable, lengthy conversation.

"I wish he'd never left," Cypress said. "They both seemed so happy. I knew this fling with that woman wouldn't last long. They had nothing in common. She was just a hot woman with perky tits that had nothing else to offer." He shook his head. "Amelia is amazing. How could he leave her?"

I smiled, liking the way Cypress defended my sister. "You're right. He was an idiot."

"The woman had his kids," he snapped. "How could he do that to her?"

"I know..."

He grabbed the mug and took a drink. "I hate Evan. Hate is a strong word and it makes me ugly, but I don't care. I hate him now, and I'll always hate him."

"I get it." I couldn't say I hated him, not when he was the father of my two nieces. That gave him a pass because he used to be a great father. He was an even more loving husband. I remembered the way he used to stare at Amelia across the table when we were all together. He couldn't care less if anyone was watching. There wasn't a doubt in my mind that he loved her, once upon a time. Obviously, lust had blurred all his logic. "So, you wanna get some breakfast, or should we whip up something here?"

"It'd be nice to be a customer at Amelia's Place for once."

"I could go for some crispy bacon and Kauai pancakes."

"Alright." His hand moved to the back of my neck, and he pulled me in for a kiss. "I'll throw some clothes on, and we'll go."

Dino bowed his head in silence and released a quiet moan.

Cypress chuckled. "He does this every time he knows I'm leaving."

"He's so smart. But we aren't leaving you behind, Dino. You wanna come with us?"

His ears perked up, and he immediately wagged his tail.

"You're so cute." I kneeled down and hugged him, getting a few wet kisses in return.

Cypress watched me from his chair, grinning at me as he watched me play with our dog. His fingertips rested against his lips, and he wore a smile that reached his beautiful eyes. "I think you're cuter."

I LEFT THE CAFÉ AND HEADED OVER TO OLIVES SINCE ACE WAS there. Cypress had been stuck to me like glue lately, so it was impossible for me to do anything without him knowing about it. As I was sworn to secrecy, I had to operate in the shadows.

I walked into the restaurant and found it in full swing. Every table was filled with people having lunch. Waiters in white collared shirts with black ties moved around and served iced tea and wine to the customers. Ace wasn't in sight, so he was probably in the back helping out in the kitchen.

I walked into the chaos of the back, where a full-time dish washer was stacking the white plates, and a waiter was looking over orders so he knew which meals to take back to his table.

Ace stood there in his slacks and collared shirt, and he sorted through the orders and handed two hot plates to the waiter so the food could get delivered faster.

"Hey, Ace."

Ace wiped his hands on the towel before he looked at me. "What's up, Bree? I didn't know you were working the lunch shift."

"I'm not. I'm at the café today."

"Then what brings you here?"

"I want to talk about Amelia. You got a minute?"

When he tensed under my stare, knowing exactly what I wanted to talk about. "I'm kinda busy right now, Bree."

"Well, with Cypress and Amelia always around, this is the only time I have."

More plates of food were placed on the rack by the chef. Ace looked at the orders before he turned back to me. "Alright. Five minutes. Go." He crossed his arms over his chest and stepped away from the rack so the waiters could move in and out better.

I suspected this would take longer than five minutes. "Evan said he wants to get back together."

Instead of pure shock spreading across his face, he held the exact same expression. "I'm aware."

"She told you?" I was surprised she told anyone besides me.

"Yeah."

"And did she tell you she wasn't going to go back to him?"

"Yes." He still wore an irritated expression, caring more about the hot food waiting to be served than a possible relationship with my sister.

"And that means nothing to you?" What was I missing? "You said you were worried she would go back to Evan, but it's obvious she's not going to. So grow some balls and tell her how you feel."

"Grow some balls?" he asked incredulously. "She says she won't go back to him now, but I'm sure after a few months, she'll change her mind."

"Then change her mind to you."

He continued to stare at me with indifference. "Why do you want me to make a move so badly?"

"Because I know how she feels about you."

"Well, when I spoke to her about Evan, she said she still loved him."

"Not in the same context."

"And you think I want to break up a family? Trust me, I wish things were different. I wish she'd never married him in the first place. If I'd done something sooner, this wouldn't be happening at all. But this is where we are. We both have to move on and accept it."

"I think you're being ridiculous."

"And I think you need to back off, Bree. I can't compete with Evan, and I'm not going to try."

"That's pathetic."

He narrowed his eyes in hostility. "She'll always love him more. I don't want to settle for less than what I deserve. That's not pathetic if you ask me."

"It's pathetic that you aren't going to even try. Come on, Ace."

"If Amelia were my wife, I wouldn't stop until I got her back. I can guarantee you Evan is going to do the same thing. Amelia is just upset right now, but when she calms down after a few weeks, he'll worm his way back into her heart. I already see it. I'll get attached to her and think everything is okay, and then she's gonna leave me for him. Not only will it hurt like hell, but it'll ruin our friendship. There'll be no coming back from that."

I crossed my arms over my chest and ignored all the employees in the back kitchen as they yelled at each other to get orders going. Steam erupted from the stove, and the place smelled like rice.

"Can you honestly tell me there's not the slightest chance she'll take him back? I was there too, Bree. I remember what they had."

I wanted to disagree with that statement but I couldn't. "I guess there's a small chance but—"

"I don't want to get involved in something complicated. Can you really hold that against me?"

"No..."

"Then drop it, Bree. It's never going to happen. Sometimes I think it could, but now that Evan is back, it can't. I know they're going to get back together. She deserves better, but I know she loves him. The girls love him. It's just the way it is." He dismissed the conversation before I could get another word in and walked away.

I could have grabbed his arm and kept the conversation going, but I knew I shouldn't. Ace made great points that I couldn't argue with. He wanted something better, to be in a relationship with a woman who didn't love another man. He was a great guy, one of the best I knew. How could I tell him he didn't deserve lasting happiness just like everyone else?

12

BLADE

I walked down the cobblestone way and entered the courtyard where the coffee shop was located. People sat at the tables with their coffee and scones, dogs lying at their feet. My heart was beating hard in my throat, and the nerves were getting to me. I hadn't spoken to Celeste in a while because I was purposely playing it cool.

But I was tired of playing it cool.

There wasn't a line today, so I walked right up to the counter. A blond woman helped me, not the person I was hoping for. "What can I get you?"

"Uh..." My eyes shifted to the door that led to the back kitchen. Celeste walked through, looking stunning in black leggings and an oversize gray sweatshirt that hung off one shoulder. Her hair was pulled into a nice bun, and she had coffee mug earrings in her lobes.

When she noticed me, she walked up to the counter with a pretty smile on her face. "I got this, Tania."

Her employee disappeared, and we were left alone together. "Here for your caffeine hit?"

"Yeah. But that's not the only reason." I purposely wore a new t-shirt that made my arms and shoulders look nice. I took more time to do my hair that morning, actually caring about someone's opinion for once.

"The scones?" she asked playfully.

Her lips tasted like scones. "You got me."

She filled a cup with medium black coffee and handed it to me. "Anything else?"

"Maybe a date tonight?" I spent every single day restraining myself from marching down here and asking her out. If I wore my heart on my sleeve, it would chase her away. Or even worse, it would bring her even closer. Both of those weren't good outcomes.

She looked at the buttons on her register. "Hmm...not sure how much that costs."

"Hopefully free."

She smiled then rang me up for the coffee. "I'd love to go out with you." She had the thickest lashes, dark and curled away from her eyes. I liked looking at them, the distinctive way they curved. She had the prettiest eyes I'd ever seen. I suddenly imagined myself on top of her in bed, my cock deep inside her as I watched every reaction she gave.

It got me hard.

I got a grip on myself. "Great. Want to get a drink at Cultura?"

"I love alcohol."

I smiled. "Me too."

"I'll see you then."

I paid for my coffee then walked away, a stupid grin on my face the entire way. When I arrived at work, they would all give me shit for it.

Like I cared.

I got to work a few minutes later and found Ace practically sleeping at his desk.

I tapped him as I walked by. "Cinderella didn't get enough sleep last night?"

Ace sat up and rubbed his eyes. "It's Sleeping Beauty, idiot."

"I'm an idiot?" I asked. "I think not knowing makes me less of an idiot."

"Well, Rose and Lily have educated me on these matters." He eyed my coffee cup and recognized the logo on the side. "Looks like you visited your French babe today."

"I did. We're going out tonight."

"Awesome. Where?"

"We're having drinks at Cultura."

"Interesting," Ace said as he rested his face against his cheek. "Cypress and I were thinking of going there."

"Not tonight," I said. "You guys need to steer clear."

"Why?" Ace asked. "Wouldn't you want your friends to meet her?"

"She's not my girlfriend and she never will be, so I don't see the point."

Ace rolled his eyes. "No need to be so serious, man. Let's just hang out and get a beer."

"It's only my second date with her. She hardly knows me, so you think she needs to know my friends?"

"Then what do you want us to do? Ignore you from across the room?"

"Just don't go there tonight."

"Free country, asshole. That's where Cypress and I are going. If you don't like it, you can go somewhere else." He walked out of the office just as Cypress and Bree walked inside. Cypress snatched my coffee off the table and took a drink. "Thanks, man."

"Not for you," I said.

"Now it is." He dropped into his chair and kept drinking it like the behavior was perfectly normal. "Pretty good. Your French babe make this?"

"Actually, yes," I answered.

"So you asked her out again?" Bree was in a cheerful mood that morning, reminding me of who she used to be before she lost her memory. "That's awesome. She sounds really great."

"Yeah, we're going to Cultura tonight but—"

"We're going there tonight too," Cypress said. "Cool, we'll get to meet her."

"No, I was just telling Ace—"

"I wanna come too," Bree said. "I can finally meet her in person."

"Finally?" I asked incredulously. "Guys, I went on one date with her."

"We can talk you up," Cypress said. "You know, tell her how awesome you are and stuff like that."

My eyes narrowed with annoyance. "We both know your idea of talking me up is telling her how I almost burned down Olives by accident."

Cypress chuckled. "Yeah, I should probably tell her that story."

"Guys, keep it cool." I left my desk and headed to the door because I knew my day wouldn't be productive if I stayed there. "I don't want to chase her off before I even get her in the sack."

"Wouldn't you like a challenge?" Cypress said. "You even said you were getting bored of the game."

"No, I'm definitely not bored of getting laid." I walked out before I could hear the happy couple say anything else. I wanted to have a quiet date with Celeste, but it would be weird if I changed our plans now. I'd just have to hope for the best.

I DIDN'T OFFER TO PICK HER UP AGAIN. IN A SMALL TOWN LIKE this, which was only one square mile, it wasn't customary to ask where someone lived. Just an awkward question all around. When I arrived at the restaurant, she was standing outside near the fire pit, looking beautiful in black leggings and a tight dress. Her hair was pulled out of her face, with dark makeup on her eyes. She wore red flats that contrasted against the dark colors she wore, and I assumed that must have been on purpose.

I walked up to her wearing a dark blue collared shirt and jeans, wanting to look nice but not overdo it. "Hey."

She was looking at her phone when I approached, so she lowered it and looked at me with that beaming smile I'd come to adore. "Hey. Right on time."

"You look nice tonight." I looked her up and down, careful not to stare at her chest longer than necessary. I'd already snuck glances when she wasn't looking, and I definitely liked the curve of her tits. They were perky, and I suspected they would be even more beautiful when she was naked. Ace and Cypress always told me they were ass men. I was definitely a tit kinda guy.

But I shouldn't get ahead of myself. If I thought about it too much, I would get hard. She had already felt my hard cock through my jeans, but I didn't want to deal with a hard-on for the rest of the night.

"Thanks. You do too." She leaned into me, rose on her tiptoes, and kissed me on the cheek.

It was classy and sexy at the time. I loved it. My arm

158   E. L. TODD

wrapped around her waist, and I guided her into the restaurant, my cock still hard without any sign of deflating. There were a few open tables in the bar, so I guided her to one by the window. The second I sat down, I heard familiar voices.

"Yo." Ace waved from across the room.

"Hey, what's up?" Cypress left his chair and grabbed his beer before he joined us at the table. "Celeste, right?" He extended his hand to shake hers.

She didn't need a moment to recover. She jumped right in. "Yeah. I'm sorry, but I don't know you."

"Your accent is awesome," Cypress blurted. "I'm Cypress, Blade's friend and business partner."

"Oh," she said with a smile. "It's a pleasure to meet you."

"I'm sure Blade didn't mention me because he hates how handsome I am," Cypress said with a straight face. "But I'm married, so he doesn't need to worry about it. Sweetheart?" He turned over his shoulder until Bree joined him. "This is my wife. Wife, this is Celeste."

I couldn't believe this was happening right now. Celeste probably thought I planned this ambush on purpose. I couldn't get mad about it, so I had to keep my cool and bite my tongue.

Bree shook Celeste's hand. "It's Bree, not wife."

Celeste laughed. "I was hoping that wasn't your actual name."

Ace came next and shook her hand. "I'm Ace. Nice to meet you."

"You too," Celeste said politely.

Ace sat down with his beer, and Cypress and Bree did the same.

I guess that meant they were sticking around.

Once they were all seated at the table, there was a long

pause of silence. Full of awkwardness, no one really knew what to say.

So I blurted something out. "I didn't plan this."

Celeste looked at me. "That's okay. The more, the merrier."

I was lucky she was being so cool about this. Not all women would go with the flow so well.

"So, you're from Paris?" Ace asked. "That's pretty cool."

"Yeah," she answered. "Born and raised. Have you ever been?"

"No," Ace answered. "I work too much."

She chuckled. "Blade said the same thing."

"All we know is work," Cypress said. "You're lucky you have a manager you can trust to look after your store while you're gone."

"It makes me uneasy sometimes, but it's definitely necessary," Celeste said. "Sometimes you need a break."

"What's that like?" Cypress asked with a laugh. "I was lucky to have Sunday off this week."

"At least we spent it wisely," Bree said.

I wished they would all disappear. They were making it so obvious that I told them everything about her. Now my heart was on display, and I couldn't keep my cards close to my vest much longer. "What can I get you to drink?"

"I'll take a gin and tonic," she said. "Thank you."

"I got it." Ace jumped out of his chair. "I insist."

"In that case, I'll take a Blue Moon," I said.

"I'm not gonna get you shit," Ace said. "Just the lady." He marched to the bar and leaned against the counter.

Celeste pressed her lips tightly together, trying not to laugh.

"Aren't my friends great?" I asked sarcastically.

"They're pretty wonderful, actually."

I didn't buy that. I left the table and ordered my own beer at the bar, ignoring Ace.

"She's cute," Ace said. "I like her style."

"Why do you think I asked her out?" I pulled out some cash from my wallet and set it on the counter.

"You're lucky you beat me to the punch." He winked before he carried the drinks back to the table. He sat down and said something funny, because everyone at the table laughed. Celeste hung out with everyone and held her ground pretty well. She was smiling and laughing with them like she wasn't uncomfortable to be there without me. She was confident and suave every time I was with her, so maybe it was just natural for her.

I carried my beer back to the table and sat down.

"We just told her about how you nearly burned Olives to the ground," Bree said.

I was seriously tempted to throw my beer on her. I gave her a cold look before I turned to my date. "I'm sure whatever version they told you was an exaggeration."

"Nope," Ace said. "It was the complete truth. He tried to microwave foil, and the place nearly burned down."

Not one of my finest moments.

Celeste rubbed her hand up and down my arm. "It's okay. I do stupid stuff all the time too."

"Yeah, right," Cypress said. "Not as dumb as this guy."

"Well, I've never almost burned down a restaurant," Celeste said. "That part is true. But I was driving around town and got lost. I was so distracted by the street signs that I hit a pole. It sucked." She shrugged it off. "Nobody's perfect."

I actually thought she was really cool for telling me that. "Thanks for coming to my rescue since my friends are determined to be jerks this evening. I'm surprised they haven't shown you any baby pictures yet."

"Actually..." Bree dug into her purse.

"No baby pictures," I said firmly. "I'll murder all of you."

"What?" Bree asked sadly. "You were so cute as a baby."

"Well, obviously," I said. "But that's not the point."

Celeste chuckled. "I mean...I wouldn't mind seeing them."

Bree grinned like a child about to get candy.

Celeste moved her hand on my thigh under the table, her fingers gripping me gently but with enough pressure to make my blood run hot.

If that was her way of persuading me, she was doing a damn good job. "Break out the photos."

WE FINALLY SAID GOODBYE TO MY FRIENDS BEFORE WE WALKED outside and inhaled the cool air that blew in from the coast. It was my second date with this woman, but I really didn't get the chance to enjoy it. I didn't get to ask her about her day, ask about her life. I was too busy dealing with the idiots I called friends.

"I'm sorry about them," I said. "I told them I was coming here tonight, so they thought it would be fun to stop by."

"They really didn't bother me." Her hand squeezed mine, her skin beautifully soft. "They were nice."

"Are we talking about the same people?"

"Oh, shut up," she said. "They're great, and you know it."

"They're great when they're being normal. That wasn't normal."

"They just care about you. I think it's cute. They wanted to scope me out and make sure I was a good fit."

"Well, I don't care about their opinion."

She smiled and came closer into my side. "You do care. And I think that's cute. You guys are like a family."

I couldn't argue with that last part, no matter how annoyed I was. "We are family." I walked her to the sidewalk before we turned and approached Ocean Street. I wanted to invite her over, but we hadn't had a very intimate evening together. Jumping into bed probably wasn't on her mind right now. "I'd like to take you out again, this time without the gang."

"That sounds nice. I'd love to."

"I'll just have to cover my tracks, make sure they don't know about the date. I know they'll crash it."

She laughed. "Now that's a little extreme."

"So, how about dinner at Casanova? It's a nice place."

"That sounds delicious." She turned around and pressed her body into me, her mouth close enough for a kiss.

After that last embrace we'd had, I wasn't walking away without another. It was the perfect memory to have when my fingers were wrapped around my cock and I was beating myself to the thought of her. I wasn't ashamed of what I did. I found this woman immensely attractive, and I wanted to fuck her the moment I laid eyes on her. The fact that I actually liked her just made me more attracted to her.

I was about to close in and kiss her when she leaned away.

"You wanna come over?"

I stilled as the blood pounded in my veins, circulating to one specific place between my legs.

"I just know when I kiss you, I'm not going to want to stop." Her lips nearly brushed against mine as she spoke. Her thick lashes covered her gaze from my view as she looked down. Since she was a foot shorter than me, I was always looking down to stare at her. It was straining on the neck but totally worth it. "My clothes are coming off...and yours are too."

Jesus Christ, that was the sexiest thing I'd ever heard a woman say to me. And with that accent...damn. She was a wet dream. My cock had never been so hard in my life. It was about to burst through my zipper. "Lead the way."

I DIDN'T CARE THAT IT WAS ONLY THE SECOND DATE. I'D picked up women in bars all my life. We did the deed and went our separate ways, both satisfied the next morning. But I'd never purposely avoided having sex with a woman because I actually liked her. The second Celeste told me she wanted to get naked together, my restraint was gone.

Hell no, I ain't saying no to that.

Her house was farther from town than my house was. The walk seemed long because we both had one thing on our minds. Her house was small and cozy with a garden blooming with roses. Once she got the door unlocked, I stepped into a beautiful French house, decorated in shades of white, gray, and black. Personal decorations were everywhere, reminding me of her native homeland. The artwork on the wall was all French landscapes, and even the smell was French, even though I had no idea what that would even smell like. A small white coffee mug sat on her coffee table, a large red lipstick mark smeared on the edge.

Her arms were around my neck instantly, her mouth pressed to mine in a heated embrace. She took charge of the situation, taking what she wanted without thinking twice about it.

I liked that.

I liked a woman who knew what she wanted and didn't wait for the guy to get on the same page. I liked her confidence. It made me even more attracted to her than I already was. My mouth moved with hers, and my hand tangled in her hair above the back of her neck. My other hand explored her waist, feeling the hourglass shape of her hips and tummy.

My lips trembled slightly as I kissed her, so aroused I could barely contain everything that I felt. I was eager and desperate, needing this woman more than I'd ever needed a woman before. I'd been single for a long time, hooking up with beautiful women and then moving on with my life. No one ever kept my attention. They weren't different or special. When I saw my friends find the people they loved, it made me feel lonely. I started to think there would never be the right woman out there for me.

But she was different.

I couldn't explain why. It was something I just knew. I think I even knew it the moment I laid eyes on her.

I backed her up into the first wall I could find and pressed her against it, using the strength of my body to pin her exactly where I wanted her to be. Now I pressed my hard cock against her, wanting to make her wet. Nothing turned on a woman more than knowing how turned on the guy was by her. I ground against her slightly, finding her clit through her dress and exerting the right pressure to make her tremble.

She wrapped one leg around my hip and rested her heel against my ass, opening herself up to me and my hard cock. Her hands explored my arms, feeling the distinct lines between my biceps and triceps. Her fingertips felt the veins of my forearms, traveling down until she felt my wrist.

She was an arm kind of woman.

Thank god I hit the gym every day.

Her nails dug into me before her hand traveled back up again, exploring me until she reached my shoulder. Her mouth never paused as she kissed me with beautiful, plump lips. I loved how they felt against my mouth, so luscious and delicious. Her lipstick had probably smeared across my mouth, but I didn't give a damn. Maybe the color would appear on my cock by the end of the night.

My phone started to ring in my pocket, but I ignored it. There was nothing that could stop me from kissing this woman. A meteor could hit the earth, and I'd still explore her mouth with my tongue.

My hands moved to her chest, and I groped both of her breasts through her dress, feeling the perky tits I'd jerked off to a few times. My thumb moved to flick over her nipples and felt them harden at my touch. I wanted to shove them into my mouth and suck them until they were raw.

Damn, she was hot.

My phone started to ring again. The only person who would call me this late would be someone in the gang. They probably had something to say about Celeste, but I didn't care about their opinion right now.

I wasn't gonna answer that phone, not if a gun was pressed to my head.

Celeste got fed up with it and yanked my phone out of my pocket. She answered it as she kept kissing me, her nails digging into my shoulder. "Blade can't come to the phone right now because he's getting laid." She hung up and shoved the phone back into my front pocket.

Goddamn, she was incredible.

I kissed her harder and carried her up the stairs to the second level. I found the closest bedroom and dropped her on the bed before I yanked my shirt over my head.

She slid to the floor and held herself on her knees. Her fingers worked my jeans and pulled them down to my ankles, my boxers coming along. My hard cock appeared, the hair on my balls trimmed because I'd hoped this might happen tonight.

I was proud of my cock, even though that made me a jackass. I was long and thick, possessing the kind of size that always hurt and pleased my women at the exact same time. I wasn't the best guy to pop a cherry because I was too big for the first time.

But for an experienced woman like Celeste, she was probably thrilled.

She tilted her head and looked up at me before she pressed her plump lips against my balls. She licked the sensitive area and made me flinch and moan at the same time. Nothing was better than having a woman's tongue against my balls.

Jesus Christ.

She licked to the base then grabbed my length and shoved it into her mouth.

Oh god.

She moved up and down my length slowly, her soaking mouth coating my skin. The grooves of her tongue felt perfect against my hardness, and I watched drops of saliva leak from the corners of her mouth. As she continued, her eyes watered in response, my dick obviously a little big for her to handle.

Where had this woman been all my life?

"Vous avez une grosse bite."

I HAD NO IDEA WHAT SHE'D JUST SAID, BUT IT WAS THE SEXIEST thing I've ever heard. Accents had never been a turn-on for me, but hearing this French babe talk to me like that was insanely arousing.

She sucked me off for another minute, using her hand to jerk me at the same time.

I wasn't going to last much longer.

I grabbed her neck and pulled my cock out of her mouth. As much as I wanted to come in that hot, warm mouth, I wanted to fuck her in a different hole. I pulled my wallet out of my jeans on the ground and found the condom I'd hidden in there. I ripped the package in half then rolled the condom onto my length.

She undressed at the same time, stripping down until she was completely naked.

Shit, her tits were perfect.

She crawled on the bed and held herself on all fours, her ass in the air and her slick pussy on display for me to view.

Beautiful pussy.

I had an out-of-body moment, watching the scene from a different angle. This was the hottest night I'd ever had in my life, and my level of arousal was making me a little insane. My cock was about to explode because it was too good to be true.

I positioned myself behind her and slid my cock into her tight pussy, feeling the tightness all the way through. I had no problem moving inside her even though my condom wasn't lubricated.

She was that wet for me.

I stopped when my entire length was sheathed.

Fuck.

She looked at me over her shoulder and started to move, her eyes locked to mine. Her dark hair cascaded down her back and between her shoulder blades. Her eyes were hypnotic as they looked into mine, staring into my soul without hesitation.

I gripped her hips and thrust into her, shoving my entire length deep inside her every time.

She gripped my forearm with her small hand, her body still turned so she could look at me. *"Plus fort."*

I didn't know a single word of French, but my instincts interpreted her meaning. I fucked her harder, digging my fingers into her skin and pounding her relentlessly. My hand moved into her hair, and I gripped it with force. I had a good hold on her, and I wasn't going to let go. As long as I was inside her, she was mine.

She closed her eyes and her mouth opened. Redness flooded her cheeks as she rode a profound high, a loud scream erupting from her throat. She gripped me tighter and moaned louder, coming around my dick with a tightness similar to an anaconda.

Now I wanted to come.

I could last longer under regular circumstances, but after that combination of French words, sexy moans, and a nail-digging grip, I was lost. I wanted to have an orgasm that rivaled hers, to crumble apart with the same ecstasy.

I leaned over her and pressed my chest into her back. I dominated her, pushing her against the bed until her stomach was against the mattress. My hips bucked harder as I pounded her into the sheets, reaching an orgasm so blinding I couldn't see for several seconds. My existence was entirely electric, feeling the greatest sensation I'd ever known. I came in the condom but pretended I was filling her bare pussy with all the come I'd just released.

It felt so damn good.

I rocked into her when I was finished, releasing any extra drops I had. My face burrowed into the back of her head, smelling her hair as well as the sweat that had collected on the back of her neck.

Now I was exhausted, drained.

I kissed the back of her neck and her right shoulder, tasting her exertion. I wanted to crawl into her bed with her and sleep off my sex-drunken state. I wanted to wake up to her the next morning, fuck her again, and then head to work.

I finally pulled out of her and excused myself to the bathroom. I unrolled the condom and did a double take when I saw how much come I'd deposited into the latex. Thankfully, I didn't break through the condom with my load.

I walked back into the bedroom and found her tucked under the sheets. Her eyes were already closed, and she hugged a pillow to her chest. She obviously had no intention of walking me out, so I assumed I was welcome to stay.

I got into bed beside her and spooned her from behind. I placed my dick right between her ass cheeks, loving how perky and soft they were. My arm circled her chest, resting right over her beautiful tits. I'd probably be hard lying beside her like this all night, but I didn't care.

It was perfect.

WHEN I WOKE UP THE NEXT MORNING, SHE WAS GONE.

I reached out to touch her soft skin, but the bed was empty beside me. Only the smell of flowers lingered behind. A second later, I heard the sound of pots and pans as well as the fragrance of freshly brewed coffee.

It was a Thursday, so I had work and so did she. I got out

of bed and threw on the clothes I'd been wearing the night before and walked downstairs.

She was already dressed for the day. Her hair was pulled back into a braid that was also flipped into a bun. She wore a long-sleeved white blouse with buttons all the way up the front, denim skinny jeans, and brown leather sandals.

Maybe it was just because she was making food, but she looked even more beautiful than she did last night—when she was naked. Bacon sizzled in the pan, and a plate was stacked high with fluffy pancakes.

She was my dream woman.

"You're awake." She set down the spatula and beamed at me with that smile that was more breathtaking than the morning sun.

"I smelled something good." My arms moved around her waist, and I pressed my forehead to hers in a greeting. "And not just you."

She leaned in and kissed me before she slid from my grasp. "I hope you're hungry."

I patted my stomach. "Just assume I'm always hungry."

"I've got pancakes and bacon. Would you like syrup and powdered sugar?"

"Yes and yes."

She finished the last touches then carried everything outside to the sand-colored picnic table. There wasn't a cloud in the sky, and the sun shone down right on us. The ocean breeze was absent that morning, making it much warmer than it usually would be at this time of day.

I sat across from her and couldn't stop staring. I had a hot plate of food in front of me as well as a steaming mug of coffee, but I didn't care about either of those things. All I cared about was the beautiful woman sitting across from me.

She held her mug with both hands and blew the steam away. "What?"

I couldn't tell her what I was really thinking, so I said something else. "Thanks for making this."

"Cooking is my passion. I don't mind." Her own plate contained a single pancake and one slice of bacon. Mine was a mound of food that could barely fit on the white plate.

I began to eat with my fork and watched her open a foreign newspaper. When I glanced at the top, I realized everything was written in French. She must keep up on the news of her mother country even when she was away. "What did you say to me last night?"

"I don't understand your meaning."

"When we were in bed together. You said a few things in French." I didn't need to know the translation to think it was sexy. Whatever her response was, it was still the sexiest thing I'd ever heard. I'd done dirty-talk, role-playing, the whole nine yards. But nothing compared to that.

"Oh..." She smiled, and her cheeks filled with color. "It doesn't matter."

Now I really wanted to know. "Come on, baby. You can tell me." I set my fork down and leaned my elbows on the table, silently pressuring her with my proximity.

"I wasn't really thinking last night. I was lost in the moment." Her cheeks were still red, and she couldn't stop smiling.

"Whatever your answer is, I thought it was insanely hot. I could listen to you talk to me like that all day."

Now her smile got bigger. "In that case..."

I held my breath as I waited.

"The first thing I said was...you have a big dick."

Man, I was hard again. She had been sucking my dick when she said that to me. The image of her on her knees played in my mind all over again. Tears burned in her eyes because her throat was barely big enough to contain me.

"And the second thing I said was...harder."

I'd definitely have to fuck her before I went to work. "That's hot."

"Yeah?" she asked. "I know I came on a little strong. That's just how I am."

"And I never want you to change."

She smiled again before she turned her gaze back to the newspaper.

I watched her now that her gaze was averted. I ate at the same time, enjoying a breakfast that rivaled the stuff we made at Amelia's Place. That tasted like crap in comparison. This woman was a million times more awesome than I initially thought.

Shit.

I WALKED INTO THE OFFICE, AND EVERYONE WAS ALREADY there.

Ace grinned at me. "Nice outfit."

"Someone had a good time last night," Cypress teased.

"She was hot," Bree said. "If I were a dude, I'd date her."

"I can't believe I missed it," Amelia said. "I love my kids, but they really encroach on my personal life."

I walked to my desk and sat down, but I wasn't happy like I had been when I first woke up that morning. I crashed —and I crashed hard. "I'm screwed, guys. I'm totally screwed."

"Why?" Bree asked. "What happened? Did you get in a fight?"

"Is she a psycho?" Ace asked. "Women get that way after sex. Become clingy and shit."

"Does she have a weird doll collection?" Cypress asked.

They totally had the wrong idea. "No. She's fucking awesome. She's absolutely perfect. She's, like, the perfect woman."

Cypress's face fell in confusion. "And that sucks because...?"

"Because you wish she were a freak who was obsessed with dolls?" Ace asked.

"Are you intimidated by a strong, successful woman?" Bree asked incredulously. "Because that's stupid, Blade."

Now they were a bunch of idiots. "It sucks because I can't have her. She was reading a French newspaper this morning. Paris will always be her home, and this place is just a vacation to her. I'm a fling and nothing more. I'll never be anything more." I hardly knew this woman, but the more I spent time with her, the more I liked her. But I didn't want to keep liking her, not when I knew how it would end. She would go back to France for six months and forget about me. When she returned, she might call me up again as a fuck buddy.

But I didn't want to be a fuck buddy.

"Oh..." Bree's face fell when she realized my problem was the opposite of her previous assumption.

"Sorry, man," Cypress said. "That is a bummer."

"I've never had a problem just being a hookup for a woman," I said. "I've been doing it all my adult life. But for some reason, it's impossible with this girl."

"How was the sex?" Ace asked.

I wouldn't share the details with anyone else outside the gang. It wasn't gentlemanly. But since we were so sickly codependent on each other, it was difficult to keep secrets. "Best I've ever had."

"Really?" Cypress said. "Even better than that one chick who was into bondage?"

"Yep," I said. "She talked dirty to me in French."

"Ooh..." Ace grinned. "That does sound hot."

Amelia snapped her head in his direction and stared at him.

"Wait, did it ever occur to you that Celeste could be feeling the exact same way?" Bree asked. "Maybe she's falling for you too and is wondering if she could even go back to Paris and leave you behind."

That would be nice. "We've only been on two dates."

"But she already slept with you," Ace pointed out. "Women do that when they like you."

"Or it could be just a fling to her," I said. "Which is what I'm thinking."

"You won't know until you ask," Cypress said. "Maybe you should ask."

I wasn't a moron. "I'm not asking her that. Again, we've been on two dates. If I bring this up and she doesn't feel the same way, I'm gonna look like an obsessed psychopath."

"True," Bree said. "You should see her for a while before you bring it up. Give her more time to fall for you if she hasn't already."

I leaned back into my chair and gripped my skull with both hands. "Why couldn't I just find some normal chick who lives around here? Why did it have to be this French babe?"

"You probably fell for her because she is a French babe," Ace observed.

"No." I remembered how I felt before I even spoke to her.

"The second I looked at her, I was into her. I just didn't expect her to be so cool. Why couldn't she be local?"

"I wouldn't say all hope is lost," Amelia said. "If you give her a reason to stay, she probably will stay. She does have a business here."

"And she has a business there," I pointed out. "So she'll always need to go back."

"But visiting for a few weeks and then coming home isn't a big deal," Cypress said. "You'd be able to get through that."

"I'll feel her out," Bree said. "Kinda just nudge her to get some answers."

"You know what I think?" Ace asked. "You're getting way ahead of yourself here. There hasn't been enough time to make any assumptions. I say you keep seeing her and just see where it goes. Maybe it doesn't go anywhere. But maybe it does go somewhere. The longer you spend time with her, the more obvious her intentions will become. If you start asking questions and lay out these expectations, it's gonna feel like a relationship. Women don't like to be caged until they're ready. And judging from the way you described her, she needs her freedom and independence. When a woman nags us to know if we're gonna be exclusive, we hate it, right?"

I nodded in agreement.

"True," Cypress said.

"So, just chill," Ace said. "That's my best advice."

"Even if I get my heart broken?"

Ace shrugged. "Whatever happens, happens. You'll just have to accept that."

13

AMELIA

Evan found any excuse to come over and see the girls. Sometimes I wondered if it was all an act just to spend time with me. Of course, that pissed me off. He shouldn't use his girls to make a pass at his wife.

I mean, ex-wife.

But he didn't bring up the idea of us getting back together again. That subject seemed to be buried in the past. We'd had the awful conversation at my kitchen table, and it seemed to die then and there.

Maybe that meant he'd given up.

I certainly hoped so.

Ace and I didn't see each other much during the week. We didn't talk to each other either. That last conversation we had in my front yard had gnawed at me ever since he'd walked away. I was paranoid that something had pushed him away. My feelings hadn't changed, so I hoped his hadn't either.

Evan picked up the girls and took them to the movies in

Monterey. A new Disney movie had just hit the big screen, and the girls were excited to see it. Of course, Evan asked me to go, but I turned him down. I'd taken those girls to enough kid movies to last a lifetime. It was nice having alone time since he'd started taking his fatherly responsibilities seriously. It was the only reason I would ever consider taking him back—having a free babysitter.

Once they were gone, I texted Ace. *The girls are gone, and I'm home alone.*

The three dots didn't light up the screen. I knew he wasn't working tonight because he handled the lunch shift at the restaurant. He could be doing a lot of other things. It didn't mean he was ignoring me.

But being the obsessed woman that I was, I stared at the phone and waited for the dots to pop up.

A minute later they did. *I can swing by.*

Maybe I was overanalyzing it, but *swing by* made it sound like he wasn't going to be around for very long. But if this was just a hookup, it shouldn't last more than an hour. Yeah, I was reading too much into it. *Great.*

He came to the house less than ten minutes later. He walked inside without knocking, making himself at home because he was entitled to. He was in snug jeans that fit his ass nicely, and his t-shirt highlighted his great arms. "Hey."

"Hey." I walked into his chest and kissed him, missing his affection because it'd been so long since I had it. I loved the way his stubble rubbed against my mouth when he kissed me. It was coarse and rough, but it felt good.

He kissed me back, but it was full of hesitance, like he wasn't sure if he wanted to kiss me or not. Normally, he would grab me and pin me against the counter, his powerful body rubbing against mine as we went at it.

But that didn't happen this time.

Something was definitely off. I could feel it.

He stepped back and cleared his throat.

He only cleared his throat when something was wrong. He didn't even do it when he was sick. "What's wrong?"

"There's nothing wrong," he said with a straight face. "I've just been thinking about our arrangement. It was fun for a while, but I think we should hit the brakes. Things are great now, but they'll get messy down the road. I think we should cool off."

He was dumping me.

Ouch.

That shouldn't hurt so much, but it did.

"Oh…" That was all I could come up with on the spot. I didn't want things to end, even if he never saw me as more than a good lay. He made me feel so many incredible things. He made me feel beautiful when I felt undesirable. He made me feel special when I was ordinary. I didn't want to give up that high.

Ace watched my expression and breathed a deep sigh of disappointment. "Our friendship means a lot to me. I don't want to lose it. And friends hooking up for long periods of time never ends well."

Unless it ended in marriage.

I was good at hiding my real emotions with Ace. I'd been doing it for a long time. But now it was difficult. He was taking away something I lived for. My daughters were everything to me, but I needed my own life. I needed my own hobbies, and Ace was my favorite hobby.

Ace continued to watch me, his face falling. "I'm sorry… maybe I waited too long."

"No, it'll be fine." I swallowed the pain and pushed on. "I guess I just don't want it to end, if I'm being honest. You make me feel like a woman, you know? I feel like so much more than a mom. I feel young again."

"You are young," he whispered.

"You know what I mean, Ace. You're my friend, and I'm also really attracted to you. It's nice to have a guilty pleasure, a secret I can enjoy in private. No one can judge me for it." I didn't mention my deeper feelings because that would just make him uncomfortable. I certainly didn't want to guilt him into staying with me. For all I knew, he'd met someone else, and he wanted to be with her exclusively. "But I understand. Your friendship means a lot to me too, and I could never lose it. It's smart to end the arrangement before it gets messy." When Ace finally left, I could lick my wounds as well as my pride. After sleeping together for weeks, he still didn't see me any differently. I didn't have amazing sex like that on a regular basis, and apparently, for him, sex was that great with just anybody. I'd give anything to have things be different, to have Ace move in and be a part of this family. My daughters were older now, but I'd have more kids if that was what he wanted.

But that would never happen.

Ace slid his hands into his pockets and kept staring at me. "I had fun, Amelia. You're an exceptional woman. There are very few people in my life that I view as highly as you. You're definitely not just a mom to me. You're a sexy lady. I mean that."

A smile formed on my lips. "A sexy lady."

He whistled. "Smokin'. Don't ever settle for a guy who doesn't think the same thing." He came closer to me and pulled his hands out of his pockets. His hands moved to my waist, and he pulled me in for a hug. "I'm glad we could work this out."

Now that I was in his arms, I closed my eyes and appreciated everything about the moment. I inhaled his masculine scent and rested my face against his hard chest. I loved feeling that strong heartbeat, knowing the safest place in the world was his arms. I didn't want to leave, not now and not ever. When I pictured him ending up with someone else and having a family, it broke my heart.

I wanted to be his family.

I'd have to settle for being his friend and business partner. I'd have to get over him and stop looking at him like that, not when he wasn't mine. I'd done everything I could to make something happen. I'd kissed him, told him how I felt, and hooked up with him for months. There was nothing more I could do to change his mind. I had to let him go and move on.

I finally left his arms, knowing I'd never be able to enjoy an embrace like that ever again. I forced myself to wear a smile so he wouldn't feel guilty for breaking my heart. I didn't even want him to know that he'd broken me.

Or that I was in love with him.

"Well, the girls and Evan will be back soon…" I didn't want to spend the next hour with him and have to keep up this fake smile much longer. I didn't have the energy to do it.

Ace seemed to want to leave too, knowing it would be awkward for a while until the novelty wore off. "Yeah, I should get going. I ate a lot today, and I need to hit the gym."

He could afford to skip a day. "Have fun."

"Alright." He gave me that handsome smile that usually made my panties melt before he walked out.

The second he was gone, my misery rose up in full force. It reached my eyes, seared my throat, and made me feel weak. My legs wanted to give out, and I felt like I was about to collapse. I reached the kitchen table and sank into the chair, feeling my shoulders sag forward and my chest start to heave.

I didn't regret much in my life, but I regretted losing my chance with Ace. If I'd known how he felt when we were younger, my life could have turned out differently. I didn't regret my daughters at all, but I did regret Evan.

Why couldn't I have been with Ace instead?

He was loyal, honest, and loving. He never would have hurt me the way Evan did. Even if he were unhappy, he would have worked it out with me until we got it right. He would have been honest with me, at least.

But I made a mistake.

I crossed my arms over my chest and felt the tears form in my eyes. When they were too heavy, they streaked down my cheeks and ruined my makeup. My chest heaved with the pain, and I was hit with the sudden loss. I'd only had a small piece of Ace.

But I felt like I'd lost all of him.

EVAN CAME HOME WITH THE GIRLS WHEN IT WAS BEDTIME. They were both tired even though they tried to hide it. They had matching princess dolls because Evan obviously had taken them shopping before the show.

The girls both hugged me before I put them to bed. I hoped Evan would leave while I was in the bedroom, but my gut told me he wouldn't. I wasn't in the mood to talk tonight. I hardly had the energy to smile and kiss my girls goodnight.

I walked back to the entryway and found him standing there, looking handsome in jeans and a t-shirt. It was nice to see him in street clothes instead of slacks and a tie. The casual look suited him just as well. He watched my expression and paid more attention than I would have liked. "You doing okay?"

"Yeah, I'm fine. Just had a long day." I couldn't force myself to sound cheery. I sounded like death, completely defeated.

Evan continued to watch me, not the gullible type. "I know something is wrong. I wish you would tell me."

I didn't see Evan as a friend. If I wanted someone to talk to, I would turn to Cypress or Bree. Bree was my sister, but I was so comfortable with Cypress because he used to look after me all the time. He turned into the brother I never had. "I just had a hard day."

"You were fine when I picked up the girls."

Was he a detective? "Well..." I didn't finish the sentence, not having the energy.

Evan walked up to me and moved his hands to my waist. It was the first time he'd touched me since he filed for divorce. The last woman he touched was Rebecca, but I didn't flinch away in repulsion. I was too depressed to care. "Hey, it's me," he whispered. "You know you can always talk to me—about anything."

Something deep inside my body told me I truly loved Ace. Love didn't come easy for me. I'd always been picky about the men I let into my life. Something told me we would have been incredible together, that I could have had the kind of relationship I'd always wanted if he felt the same way about me. I kept thinking about all the possibilities, and I had to remind myself harshly that I needed to let it go.

He didn't want me. End of story.

"I'm in love with Ace..." I looked into Evan's face as I said the words, not caring if the truth hurt him. He'd scarred me more times than I could count, and I didn't feel the least bit of guilt for being honest.

Evan didn't react, but I knew the words stung.

"But he doesn't want me," I whispered. "He came over tonight and broke things off."

Evan kept his hands on my body but didn't say anything.

"We were just hooking up. It was nothing serious. But I thought he would feel the way I did eventually. I told him how I felt, but he didn't feel the same. And he'll never feel the same way." I bowed my head in embarrassment. I'd just told my ex I couldn't get the guy I wanted, and that made me feel ugly and undesirable.

He moved closer to me. "He's an idiot. A big one."

I sniffed and held back the tears before they could fall again.

"If he thinks he can do better than you, he's stupid."

"Stupid like you?" I felt bad for making a jab when Evan was only trying to comfort me.

"Yeah," Evan said without offense. "You'd think the guy would learn from my mistake."

I couldn't believe I was standing in my kitchen being comforted by the man who'd left me for another woman. I didn't think I'd wind up here, ever sinking this low. But here I was, a pathetic mess.

I let Evan touch me because I didn't know what else to do. I didn't care enough to push him off. I didn't care about anything then. I judged myself for being so emotionally unstable, but I was tired of being rejected, of being second best.

Evan's hand moved to my cheek, and he directed my gaze onto his. His callused thumb brushed against my soft skin, and he looked at me in just the way he did on our wedding day. I knew he was going to kiss me.

Now was the best time to move out of the way.

But I didn't move. I stood there and let it happen.

He leaned in and kissed me, pressing his warm mouth against mine. The kiss was familiar because I would never forget how it felt to kiss the man I was married to for eight years. It was the kiss I experienced every single day before we went to work and before we went to sleep.

His hand slid into my hair, and he deepened the kiss when he knew I wouldn't object. He sucked my bottom lip into his mouth and breathed into me, his hard chest feeling incredible against mine. It was nice to feel wanted immediately after I was rejected. I felt weak, the kind of woman I never wanted to be.

But I'd hit rock bottom.

MY ALARM WENT OFF THE NEXT MORNING, AND I SLAMMED MY hand down on top of it. The sun was already shining through the windows, telling me it was going to be a warm day. I kicked off the sheets and sat up in bed, realizing Evan was still beside me.

I hadn't planned for this. Now I had Evan in the bed we slept in for eight years, and our daughters were just down the hall.

I didn't want to get their hopes up that we were getting back together. The girls would be so excited, and I would hate to shatter their dreams. I grabbed Evan and gently shook his arm. "I should let you out before the girls see you."

He sat up in bed, his hard chest strong with muscle. His shoulders and arms were cut, and he was in the best shape of his life. He'd obviously been exercising even more than he did before. He ran his fingers through his hair then wiped the sleep from his eyes. "Why can't they see me?"

"You know why, Evan." It was way too early in the morning to have this conversation.

Evan was too tired to have it either, so he got up and pulled his clothes on.

I snuck him to the front of the house and let him out the front door. "I'll see you later."

He kissed me on the mouth unexpectedly before he walked to his car at the curb.

I'd have to tell Evan last night was a one-time thing before he made any assumptions. But I couldn't worry about that right now.

I got the girls ready for school, dropped them off, and then went to work. When I walked into the office, everyone was already there. Cypress handed me a coffee right when I walked inside, always looking out for me in ways I didn't expect.

When I looked at Ace, he stared back at me with an unreadable gaze. He was stoic, telling me our conversation last night had no effect on his night. I was the only one who walked away with a broken heart.

Sleeping with Evan was such a stupid idea. I had no idea why I was so stupid. At the time, it was nice not to be alone. The sex was good, like it'd been during our marriage, and that was enough of a distraction.

But I knew there would be consequences.

"How was your night?" Bree asked.

"Good," I said, knowing Ace could hear me. "Evan took the girls to the movies, so I took a bath and had some wine." And I cried my eyes out before I slept with my ex-husband. "How was yours?"

"We took Dino on a walk at the beach then had dinner."

It seemed like she and Cypress did everything together now. That made me happy. Those two belonged together, even if Bree couldn't remember why. I was glad she'd given him another chance, and I was glad Cypress was patient enough to wait for that second chance. "What am I doing this morning? Am I at the café or downstairs?"

"You're downstairs," Blade said. "I'll head to the café."

I was glad I didn't have to spend the afternoon working with Ace. That would suck.

"I'll stay here," Cypress said. "Ace will be at Olives. Bree will be at the café. Go team."

"We aren't cheerleaders," Blade said. "Even though I'd probably look amazing in a skirt."

"With those chicken legs?" Ace asked. "I doubt it." He left the office and walked down the stairs to head to work.

Once he was out of the room, I could breathe again. Bree and Blade left for work together, so Cypress and I headed downstairs to get ready to open the diner. We placed all the chairs on the ground then Cypress took care of the register. I started brewing the coffee and threw all the oranges in the squeezer. "How are things with my sister?"

"Good," he said with his back turned to me. "We're having lots of sex, which makes me happy."

"After eighteen months without getting laid, you must be thrilled."

"Hey, I got laid a few times," he said. "So it's not like I don't have mad skills. And the sex is just as good as it used to be. You know, since she doesn't scream at me for cheating on her all the time."

"So she's finally let that go?"

"Eh." He shrugged. "Not totally. But she's not so venomous about it. When I tell her I love her, she doesn't say it back. That doesn't make me mad, but I do miss hearing her say it."

"You have to cut her some slack. In her mind, you're completely starting over."

"No, I do get it. I'm just glad I have her. I'm not gonna complain. If she looks through my phone and constantly needs to know where I am, I don't care about that either. She's entitled to her trust issues."

"I can't see her doing that."

"She hasn't. But if that will give her peace of mind, I'm all for it." He shoved the cash into the register then joined me in the kitchen. "How are things going with Evan?"

"I'm not seeing him." I immediately grew defensive, terrified someone would figure out my dirty secret.

"I never said you were. But I know he's been trying to be an actual father again. He's kept his commitment?"

Too much, actually. "He's around more than I'd like, which is a sudden change."

He shrugged. "Better than never seeing him, right?"

Not quite. "He told me what you guys did."

Cypress avoided my gaze and brushed off the comment. "Not sure what you mean."

"He told me you guys went to his office and told him to get his shit together."

Now Cypress was backed into a corner, and he squirmed. "Uh...well...yeah. We were just trying to help."

I was hurt that Ace never told me the truth, but I could never get mad at what they did. They had my best interest at heart, and I considered myself to be very lucky. "I know. When Evan told me, I was surprised."

"Shouldn't be. We always have your back. You know that, Amy." He raised his fist and held it out to me.

I smiled then tapped my fist against his. "I know, Cypress."

Cypress smiled then walked back to the register.

I turned back to what I was doing so I could hide my face. If Cypress knew I hooked up with Ace for so long and then he dumped me, he'd rip his throat out. He wouldn't be so quick to forgive again.

That was why I had to keep it to myself.

For Ace's sake.

14

I finished up at the café then headed home, knowing Cypress would already be back at the house or would be leaving work soon. Being next-door neighbors forced us to be together nearly all of the time. It had its pros and its cons.

It definitely made moving forward easier. If we weren't neighbors, it might have been easier for me to forget about him and start dating again. But how could I date someone else when I saw Cypress with his shirt off every single day? When I was greeted with that handsome smile every time we were face-to-face? When he constantly wore the wedding ring I gave him on our wedding day?

He pretty much made it impossible.

And I started to recognize the changes he'd made. He was always considerate and kind toward me, taking care of me even when I didn't have a clue who he was. He had been loyal to me every single day since we said I do.

I would never know if he'd always been faithful to me when my memory was gone, but I had to hope he had been.

It wouldn't make any sense for him to look after me every day if he wasn't that committed.

When I got to the house, there was a note on my door.

Date night. Be ready at 7.

I pulled the note off the door and read it again, a smile forming on my face. I suspected he was watching me through the window, but I didn't turn to look at him. I stuffed the note into my pocket and walked into the house, realizing I was going on my first date with my husband.

I FOUND A BLACK DRESS IN MY CLOSET WITH SEE-THROUGH lace as the sleeves. It was short and tight, and since it'd been eighty degrees that afternoon, it was the perfect day to wear it. I wore black flats because heels were simply impossible when we walked everywhere.

I did my hair and makeup and felt a jolt of excitement I hadn't experienced in a long time. It reminded me of when we were first dating years ago. He was my dream guy, and I finally got to have him. I didn't think about the way he'd cheated on me. In fact, I'd been thinking about it less and less with every passing day.

It didn't seem relevant anymore.

At seven, he arrived at my door. He was in dark jeans and a collared shirt, his shoulders looking broad in the fabric. He had just shaved his face, so his jawline was clean, revealing the prominent angles of his chin. His rugged masculinity constantly contrasted against the bright blue color of his eyes. It was the only traditionally pretty feature he possessed.

He took a look at my figure in my dress, his gaze taking in every single feature. He gave me two thumbs up when he was finished. "You look sexy as hell. I like this." He moved into my body and circled my waist with his large hands, pressing me back into the door like he had no intention of taking me anywhere. His hands gripped the fabric of my dress, bunching it up until the bottom part of my ass was sticking out. "I really like this."

When he was this close to me, I could feel his erection through his jeans. I suspected it hadn't been there a second ago. "I can tell."

"Are you sure?" He spoke against my mouth, nearly touching me. "I can show you if you'd like."

"After you buy me dinner."

He chuckled. "A woman who knows what she wants...I like it." He finally gave me what I'd been waiting for and kissed me on the mouth. Despite his having a shaved face, the skin around his mouth was still slightly coarse and rough. I liked the way it felt. I liked the way it felt between my thighs too.

When I felt those nice lips, I didn't care about dinner. I wanted to eat him instead.

Cypress ended the embrace before it could escalate any further. Whenever our mouths were pressed together, an atomic explosion erupted between us. Maybe trust hadn't developed yet, but we certainly had the right chemistry. "We should get going. Otherwise, we're gonna order a pizza in the nude."

"Doesn't sound so bad."

He grinned then pulled me along. "Don't tempt me."

THERE WAS A NEW STEAKHOUSE ON DOLORES AND 7TH, AND ironically, that was the name of the restaurant. I'd walked by it countless times and assumed it was an art gallery because the floor plan didn't resemble any restaurant I had ever seen. It was a perfect square, with large floor-to-ceiling windows and European furniture inside.

Cypress and I had a table in the center of the room, and other couples sat nearby, drinking wine and enjoying the fresh bread and butter. I ordered a sirloin, and Cypress did the same even though neither one of us ate much red meat. I'd always been a fish sort of person.

We each sipped on the wine and looked at each other across the table, both lacking our usual conversation skills. Every interaction I had with Cypress up until that point had been at our houses or at work.

We hadn't been both intimate and public at the same time.

"Our first date..." I ripped a piece of bread from the loaf and dropped it into my mouth.

"Yeah, our hundredth first date," he said with a chuckle. "We've had a lot of first kisses too."

"I wonder how many."

His eyes shifted back and forth as he counted them over the past eighteen months. "About thirty."

"Wow. That's a lot."

He shrugged. "I'm a pretty smooth guy."

I rolled my eyes. "If you're smooth, you're humble."

"I am humble," he said. "I was married to you, so I had the upper hand."

"If I'm not aware of the legal binding, it doesn't count."

"Whatever. Most men wouldn't have been able to make it happen. Whenever you woke up on the right side of the bed, I was there. I flirted, I complimented, and I got you into bed. I think it had something to do with your hormones too, around your monthly cycle."

I blanched at the thought that Cypress knew my menstrual cycle better than I did.

"At that time of the month, I didn't interact with you at all unless I had to," he said with a chuckle.

"You wouldn't have wanted to get laid at that time anyway."

He chuckled. "No, I definitely would. Period or no period, makes no difference to me."

I cringed in disgust even though it was my body we were talking about. "So, we would do that when we were married?"

"Every day," he said. "The only times we wouldn't was when either one of us was really sick. Now, that's just gross."

We had different definitions of gross.

"Anyway." He held up his glass of wine and tapped it against mine. "To our first date."

"Our first date." I drank my wine then set it on the white tablecloth. "How are your parents doing?"

"They're good. They were really excited when I told them you were doing well."

"That's great." I had no idea what these people even looked like. I didn't meet them when we dated the first time. Kinda strange. "I guess I'll have to meet them all over again..." I got nervous at the thought of meeting my in-laws, terrified they wouldn't like me. But I'd already made my first impression, so there was nothing I could do about their opinion now.

"They love you more than they love me," he said with a chuckle. "So you don't need to worry about anything. My mother thinks I'm a dumbass. And she's glad that you love me even though I'm a dumbass."

I smiled, liking his mother already. "Do they know we dated before?"

He nodded. "I told them what happened. Another reason why my mother thinks I'm a dumbass."

I was surprised he'd told them that and dragged his own name through the mud. But I also respected his honesty. "You have a brother too, right?"

"Pine," Cypress said. "He thinks you're hot."

Both of my eyebrows rose. "And you're fine with that?"

"I'm hotter than he is, so I have nothing to worry about."

"There goes that arrogance again..."

"I'm just a confident guy. I know what I have to offer a woman. And I also know when a woman is into me. My wife is definitely into me."

I did make it pretty obvious as much as I tried to act distant. "Well, if you keep being this confident, you may not get laid tonight."

"Oh, I'm getting laid. I'll liquor you up more if I have to, but I'm getting some action."

I squeezed my thighs together under the table, knowing I would cave the second we got home. I might have to walk around in my house naked and hope he watched me through his windows, enticing him to come over.

Cypress drank from his glass and stared at me hard, his thoughts obviously on sex. I could tell just by looking at him. Spending every single day with him for the past few months had taught me how to decipher every word and every action.

I felt like prey being the subject of his gaze, but in a way I liked. I liked his bossy authoritativeness. Somehow, he pulled it off when other guys couldn't. There was something about him that made me love everything, even his flaws.

I squeezed my legs tighter together and felt all my nerves fire off. I wanted to defuse the intensity of the situation since we still had to get through the rest of dinner. This first date wasn't going the way it should. We wanted to skip all the bases and slide into home plate right away. "Excuse me..." I walked away and headed into the bathroom, giving myself a second to cool down. I needed to use the bathroom anyway, so I did my business and washed my hands. Just a month ago, I'd decided this wasn't going to work with Cypress. I'd had every right turning my back on him, but in the end, that wasn't what I wanted. My heart had loved him since the first time I laid eyes on him, and that kind of affection would never die. My instincts told me that if a man cheated once, he would do it again. But my heart disagreed.

I believed in him.

I walked back into the restaurant and found a woman sitting in the chair I had vacated. Her back was to me, and she had bright blond hair and a slender figure that was a few sizes smaller than mine.

My initial response was fury. I wasn't the jealous type, but I was certainly insecure after what Cypress had done.

But I reminded myself that I didn't want to be that person—not anymore. I was always calm and confident, and I wouldn't let any supermodel make me feel intimidated. She was probably a local or a restaurant acquaintance. Any decent woman wouldn't hit on a married man the second his wife walked into the bathroom.

Cypress looked up at me, and instead of wearing that calm smile I was used to seeing, he looked uncomfortable.

Awkward.

Different.

When I reached the table, I looked down at the woman paying him a visit. The second I saw her face, I recognized her.

Like I could ever forget such a skank.

Vanessa.

His ex.

The woman he cheated on me with.

And she was sitting in my seat.

"Hey." She gave me the fakest smile I'd ever seen, obviously confident that she'd seduced Cypress when he was committed to me. She didn't feel any remorse at all. And the fact that she was sitting across from him told me she wasn't done with him.

That she would never be done with him.

I felt so much rage. I couldn't contain it all. The last time I was this pissed was when I walked in on Cypress while he was fucking her. I could grab the glass of wine and throw it in her face. Shit, I should break the bottle over her skull.

But I didn't do that, keeping my head held high and controlling the situation. "Hey." That was all I could spit out right then.

Cypress cleared his throat. "My wife and I were just having dinner. It was nice to see you, Vanessa, but our entrees will be here any second." He rose out of his chair and came to my side, physically choosing sides so there was no misinterpretation.

Vanessa brushed it off with a smile. "Of course. I'll see you around." She got out of the chair, showing off her flawless figure in a skintight dress. She gave a beautiful smile that was only reserved for Cypress.

All the happiness I'd had just moments before vanished.

She walked to the other side of the room where her table sat. Another woman of the same age was with her. They were probably two friends who decided to go out for a drink and a meal.

I moved away from Cypress and sat down, not exploding the way I wanted to in order to save face in front of Vanessa. If she knew her little charade got under my skin, she would win. So I sat down and took a long drink of my wine.

Cypress moved into the other seat, his shoulders slumped and his eyes lidded like he was tired. He rubbed the back of his neck and sighed, as if he was on the verge of falling asleep right at the table.

Thankfully, the waiter arrived and placed the dishes in front of us, giving us something to do other than sit in awkward silence. I avoided eye contact, so I wasn't sure if he was staring at me. He probably was.

We started eating, and I forced the bites down my throat. I was hungry at the beginning of the evening, but now I felt like I could throw up. The food was tasteless even though it was obviously exquisite. All the bile had risen up into my throat and burned my taste buds away.

Cypress ate, but he didn't seem impressed by the food.

Would it be totally rude if I asked for the check?

I kept my gaze down and tried to get through the meal, but time seemed to be passing so slowly. The encounter with Vanessa kept playing over and over in my mind, and I couldn't swallow the hurt it caused. Seeing her only reminded me of what she did. She obviously thought she and Cypress were friendly, and that made the paranoia set in.

Did he sleep with her while he was married to me?

The fact that I wasn't sure stung.

The fact that I didn't trust him was painful.

Seeing her only reminded me of what Cypress did, of how he broke my heart on that horrific night. If I didn't think about it, it didn't seem so bad. But now that Vanessa was still real, still friends with Cypress, it made me realize she would never go away.

And I would never trust him.

WHEN WE LEFT THE RESTAURANT AND WALKED OUTSIDE, THE cool evening breeze was a gulp of fresh air. It evaporated the sweat that had formed on the back of my neck. Cypress's arm circled my waist, and I didn't push it away, hoping Vanessa saw it from her seat in the restaurant.

Cypress and I hadn't said more than a few words to each other. He must have known it was stupid to provoke me in the middle of the crowded room with the whore still present. Only when we were alone together could the real conversation happen.

We walked down the hill until we arrived at our two houses sitting quietly on the dark street. The sun had set an hour ago, so there was little light to navigate with. It was one of the rare times my mind was completely blank. I was usually thinking in some capacity, but now there wasn't a single thought going through my brain.

I shut down.

Cypress sighed before he spoke. "She came over to say hi to me. I didn't know she was there until she sat down."

I crossed my arms over my chest as I looked at him, unable to ask the question that was gnawing at me.

"She means nothing to me."

But she meant enough to cheat on me. "You guys keep in touch?"

"No, not really."

"It seemed like she thought you were friends, so you've obviously talked to her." I accused him in the most delicate way possible, not wanting to explode the way my heart already had.

"She's come into the restaurants a few times since she lives around here. But that's it."

I still couldn't ask. A part of me didn't want to know. And another part of me wasn't sure if I could believe him even if he said no.

Cypress stared at me with his hands in his pockets. He didn't look angry or annoyed, just afraid. I'd never seen him look like that before, restrained and silent.

I couldn't keep it in any longer. My mouth wouldn't retain the words, and my chest had already cracked in two. "Did you sleep with her while you were married to me?" My voice was so quiet I wouldn't blame him if he didn't hear me.

"No."

I took a deep breath, and the cold air burned my lungs.

"I didn't." He sighed, either in disappointment or sadness.

"You were alone for eighteen months. How can I expect that to be true?"

"If I'd slept with her, I would tell you," he said calmly.

"Not when we're on the rocks."

His eyes narrowed. "I fucked up one time. But I've never lied. So don't punish me for a crime I never committed. I'll tell you whatever you want to know. I'm an open book, sweetheart."

"So you were never with a single person in that period?"

"No."

"You never slept with anyone?"

"No."

"You never kissed anyone?"

Cypress closed his eyes, dead silent.

Now my heart really was broken. "So you were with someone?"

"I didn't sleep with anyone. It was nothing. Not even worth mentioning. I'm only bringing it up because you directly asked."

"And you didn't mention this before?"

"Again, you never directly asked."

"Wow, you're an asshole."

He closed his eyes again, his jaw clenching.

"You kissed Vanessa?"

"No," he said quickly. "I haven't touched her since the day you were in my life again. I've hardly looked at her."

I wanted to believe him. He'd just confessed something else, so why would he lie about her? "Who did you kiss?"

"It doesn't matter. It happened one time, and it lasted thirty seconds before it was over."

"If it doesn't matter, why did you kiss her?"

He looked at the houses, refusing to make eye contact with me.

"Cypress."

"What?" he whispered. "It didn't mean anything to me—"

"It didn't mean anything when you fucked Vanessa either. It seems to be a pattern with you, cheating on your wife with women who don't matter. Then I must not matter."

"That's not how it is."

"Who did you kiss, Cypress?" Why wouldn't he tell me?

"Because it doesn't matter," he repeated.

"You cheated on me—again. It does matter."

"I didn't cheat on you."

"Kissing another woman constitutes as cheating. It doesn't matter if it was thirty seconds or thirty minutes." I felt stupid for taking a chance on him when I knew it would never work. Now we were back to where we were, me hating him. I thought we could work this out, but I was stupid for ever having that fantasy. I was an idiot for thinking that dream could ever come true. "Cypress, I'm done. This isn't going to work out, and we both know it. I tried. I really did. But I'm never gonna feel secure in this relationship. And now that you've also kissed someone...you disgust me." Tears burned behind my eyes, but I didn't let them fall. I wasn't crying over this man anymore.

"I'm telling you, this kiss wasn't anything great. It was meaningless and uncomfortable. It doesn't count."

"It doesn't count?" I asked incredulously. "Yes, it does count."

"Your imagination is far worse than what really happened."

"Then why don't you just tell me exactly what happened? And exactly who it was with?"

He still didn't give me an answer.

"Does she work for us?"

Nothing.

"Is she a regular at one of our restaurants?"

Not a peep.

"Or is it really Vanessa?"

"It's not her," he repeated.

"If this is so meaningless, why didn't you tell me in the first place?"

"Because I'm not a liar," he snapped. "Yes, my lips touched someone else's. You asked, and I told you. But it wasn't sexual. It wasn't intense. It happened, and then it was over. It never should have happened in the first place."

"But yet, you did it anyway." I was finished with this man. I no longer had a single drop of hope. All we could ever be at this point was friends. And even that I was unsure of. "I'll talk to a lawyer tomorrow and get those divorce papers ready. You can't change my mind this time, Cypress. I gave this relationship a try, and now I'm certain it'll never work. Respect my wishes, and let it go."

He stood across from me without moving. He didn't say a single word or come closer to me.

I turned to my house and walked up the stairs, feeling worse than I had when I'd first gotten my memory back. I was more desolate, more depressed than before. Cypress wasn't someone I could trust. My own husband betrayed me —twice. He might be beautiful, kind, and generous, but he wasn't the kind of man to keep it in his pants.

He was a manwhore.

Cypress didn't object to my exit. He didn't say he wasn't going to give up on us. He just let me go, knowing there was no reason to fight.

Because there was nothing left to fight for.

15
———

AMELIA

A knock sounded on the door while I was making dinner in the kitchen. I hadn't spoken to Evan since he spent the night, and I suspected he was the one dropping by. Ace and I hadn't communicated with each other outside of work, so I doubted he would drop by anytime soon. The wound was still too fresh, the awkwardness still heavy.

I opened the door, and sure enough, Evan was standing there.

He was in jeans and a hoodie, looking more handsome than usual because I knew how hard his body was under those clothes. "Hey. Am I interrupting anything?" He held a bottle of red wine.

"The girls and I were just about to have dinner."

"Can I join you?" He held up the bottle. "I got this Bordeaux for you." He turned the bottle so I could read the label.

It was the same wine and the same year that we used for our wedding.

As if that was a coincidence.

When I hesitated, he invited himself inside. "What are you making?"

I knew he and I were going to have to speak about this eventually, so we may as well get it over with. "Meat loaf."

"Ooh...sounds amazing. I miss your meat loaf." He opened the bottle of wine at the counter and poured two glasses. "Hey, girls."

"Hey, Dad." Rose waved from her spot at the table right beside Lily.

"Daddy's gonna eat with us?" Lily asked.

"Yes, princess." Evan set the two wineglasses down and sat at the head of the table, exactly where he used to sit before he ruined our marriage.

I felt like he was purposely manipulating me with the past, reminding me of the happiest moments of my life. I had plenty of food, so I served him a plate then took my seat. The girls were obviously happy having both of us at the dinner table. Rose kept asking Evan about his day then asked if he would buy her a turtle.

She was not getting a turtle.

"You'll have to ask your mother," Evan said, giving the right answer.

"But she already said no," Rose said. "And I don't like that answer."

Evan laughed. "That's too bad. Looks like you aren't getting a turtle."

"How about a puppy?" Lily asked. "We love puppies."

"Nope," I said. "When you guys are older, we'll talk about it." I was already overwhelmed being a single mom with two kids. Throw in a puppy that needed to be potty trained, and I would lose my mind.

Rose's face fell in sadness. "Mommy never lets us do anything..."

"Mommy is mean," Lily whispered.

These were the moments when I hated being a mom. My children were too young to understand everything I did for them, that I never faltered in taking care of them even when my world was ripped apart. They'd always been the center of my universe no matter what. But no matter what I did, I wasn't good enough. I drank my wine, taking the biggest gulp I could without choking.

"Your mother isn't mean," Evan said firmly. "She's the best mom in the world, and you know it. Who makes you breakfast every morning? Who takes you to school and picks you up every day? Lily, what would you do if Mom didn't show up one day? Where would you go? Do you know how to get home on your own?"

Lily picked at her food with her fork, her eyes downcast.

"Rose." Evan's authoritative voice rose in the room. "What would you do if Mom didn't help you with your math homework? Would your teacher be happy about that? Would you get a check minus?"

Rose didn't have anything to say to that.

"Never say your mother is mean again," Evan continued. "She's always been there for you. Always." He looked down at his food and didn't meet my look.

I was touched by the speech because it didn't feel staged. It seemed genuine, as though he wasn't just trying to get into my good graces again so we could get back together. He finally gave me the credit I was due and admitted to being an inadequate father—to his own kids.

It definitely made me look at him differently.

———

Evan helped me clear the table and load the dishes into

the dishwasher. Then he got the girls to brush their teeth and get ready for bed. Once they were tucked in for the night, he joined me in the kitchen.

I started the dishwasher then washed my hands in the sink. I looked out the window and tried not to meet his gaze, afraid of having any kind of intimacy with him. I dried my wet hands with a towel then finally turned around. "Thanks for saying that."

He leaned against the opposite counter, facing me. "It needed to be said. It's true."

"That's the only thing I hate about being a mother. They never appreciate me."

"Only for now," he said. "When they get older, they'll understand. And when they're adults, they'll be your friend. You aren't the only parent to go through this."

"I hope you're right." Rose was only seven. I had ten more years to go before she became an adult. And even then, she still probably wouldn't be mature enough.

"You're a great mom. Of course, I'm right." He gave me an encouraging smile as he held on to the counter behind him. His hair was done well that afternoon, and the hoodie he wore emphasized his body even though the muscles were covered.

I waited for him to leave, but he obviously had no intention of going anywhere. I had to have the dreaded conversation with him, to tell him our hookup couldn't happen again. I had just been depressed and stupid. "I know we got carried away the other night, but I don't think we should allow it to happen again." I kept my voice steady as I spoke, hoping he would receive the message well.

He continued to stare me down, his gaze unreadable.

"I want to be friends and partners, but that's it. I don't want anything else."

Evan walked toward me, moving past the empty barrier between the kitchen counters.

I held my breath, forcing myself not to respond to his proximity.

"I think you want more than that."

"I don't." I looked him in the eye as I said it. "I was just depressed about Ace, and I wasn't thinking clearly."

"You used me to stop thinking about him. Why don't you use me to get over him?"

Both of my eyebrows rose at the offer. "You want to sleep with me even though I'm in love with someone else?" How could that not wound his pride? How could that not disgust him?

"I think that's fair after what I did. I can be patient." His hands moved to either side of the counter, and he pressed farther into me, his face lowering toward mine. "I can make love to you until I'm the only man you think of."

I was still attracted to Evan. That much was obvious. But I hadn't forgiven for him what he did. I would never trust him again. The only reason he was still in my life at all was because he was the father of my children.

He leaned in to kiss me.

If I didn't stop it, it would happen again. It would be another mistake that I would regret in the morning. I pressed my hand against his chest and steadied him. "No."

He grabbed my hand and intertwined our fingers before he pressed his lips against mine. "Yes."

MY PHONE WOULDN'T STOP RINGING ON THE NIGHTSTAND. I had no idea what time it was, but it was way past my bedtime. I fumbled in the dark until I finally found the phone next to my alarm clock. I answered the call without looking at the screen and kept my eyes closed. "Hmm?"

Evan turned over and faced the other direction, trying to get away from the sound of my voice.

"I'm sorry to wake you," Bree said into the phone. "I'm standing outside."

"Why?" I said with a cracked voice. "Everything okay?"

"I need to talk to you. I'm sorry for bothering you so late, but it's important."

"No, it's okay." I kicked the covers back and sat up in bed. "I'll be right there." I hung up and returned the phone to the nightstand. After I pulled on my pajama bottoms and a t-shirt, I walked to the front door. I didn't bother putting on a bra because I was too tired. Bree wouldn't care. She'd seen me naked more times than either of us cared to admit.

I opened the door and let her inside. "Hey, what's going on?"

Bree flipped on some of the lights before she walked into the living room and sat down. "Cypress and I were having dinner tonight..."

I took the seat beside her, my eyes wide open now that I was looking at her. The second she said it was important, my body kicked into gear and I became wide awake. My sister wouldn't stop by in the dead of night if it weren't important. I glanced at the time on the TV receiver and saw it was only eleven.

Damn, I was lame.

"What happened, Bree?"

"I went to the bathroom at a restaurant, and when I came back to the table, Vanessa had taken my seat."

That cunt was back? "Oh no..."

"She said bye to Cypress then returned to her seat on the other side of the restaurant. Seeing her just made me angry all over again. It felt just like it did when I caught Cypress fucking her." Spit flew from her mouth because she was so pissed. "It made me feel all the things I hate to feel, and right then, I didn't think it would work. Cypress and I had made a lot of progress, but all of that went out the window when I saw her."

"You can't get mad at Cypress for running into her. That wasn't his fault. Just a terrible coincidence."

"Well, when we got home, I asked if he'd ever been with her while we were married. He said no."

Of course he did. "Cypress was loyal to you, Bree. I know that's hard to believe, but it's true."

"Then I asked if he'd ever been with anyone, and he said no. Then I asked if he'd even kissed anyone...and that's when he said yes."

My heart sank into the pit of my stomach. "He said yes?"

"He said it didn't mean anything, and it wasn't worth counting. But if it wasn't meaningful, then why did it happen at all? He refused to tell me who he kissed or how it happened. Honestly, the details don't matter. It's not hard not to kiss someone. He obviously has a problem with fidelity and loyalty, and he'll never change. So I said we're through. I have no idea why I was so stupid to marry him in the first place, but I'm not repeating that same mistake."

My heart was beating so fast I could hardly breathe. "And what did Cypress say to that?"

"Nothing. He let me go."

Anxiety rushed through my body, and I started to sweat. I couldn't think straight because terror gripped me by the throat. Everything was crashing down around me, and I didn't know how to stop it.

Bree shook her head and looked across the living room. "I feel so stupid..."

Not as stupid as I did.

She ran her fingers through her hair and sighed, still pissed off as hell.

I tried to think of the right thing to say, but I choked. When I was put on the spot, I couldn't confess the truth. I couldn't tell her what happened that night. I was too afraid of what would result.

I was too afraid that I would lose my sister.

Because I was the one who'd kissed Cypress.

Footsteps sounded a second later, and Evan appeared from the hallway in his jeans and t-shirt, his hair messy and his eyes heavy with sleep.

Why was this happening?

Bree stared at him in shock, her eyes popping wide open in horror.

God, this was bad.

Evan looked at her awkwardly before he turned to me. "Just wanted to make sure everything was okay."

I couldn't say anything.

Bree turned to me, both of her eyebrows so high it looked like they would jump off her face.

So bad.

Evan walked back down the hallway. I heard the front door click when it was closed.

Bree kept staring at me, her look full of accusation.

I didn't say anything, knowing any comment I made would just make me look worse.

Bree obviously didn't know what to say because her expression kept changing, kept hardening.

I was in deep shit.

ALSO BY E. L. TODD

Find out how the story ends in 218 First Hugs.

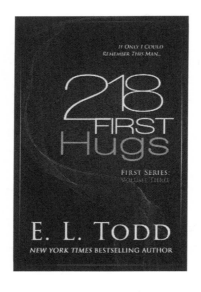

AFTERWORD

Dear Reader,

Thank you for reading 325 First Fights. I hope you enjoyed reading it as much as I enjoyed writing it. If you could leave a short review, it would help me so much! Those reviews are the best kind of support you can give an author. Thank you!

Wishing you love,

E. L. Todd

ABOUT THE AUTHOR

Subscribe to my newsletter for updates on new releases, giveaways, and for my comical monthly newsletter. You'll get all the dirt you need to know. Sign up today.

www.eltoddbooks.com

Facebook:
https://www.facebook.com/ELTodd42

Twitter:
@E_L_Todd

.

Made in the USA
Lexington, KY
27 September 2017